SEARCH FOR A PAST

"Who"—Dave stared up at him groggily—"who are you?"

"I'm Lance! Don't you remember me, your brother, Lance? Dave, you've got to remember me!"

My brother! Dave shook his head, trying to clear the dizziness, to break through the cloudy curtain that hung there. My brother! We must have spent a lot of years together, played ball, helped each other out of scrapes. There was a past life, other places, other people—and I don't remember it. *Dear Lord, why?*

They Never Came Home

Lois Duncan

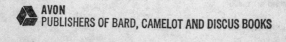

AVON
PUBLISHERS OF BARD, CAMELOT AND DISCUS BOOKS

All the characters in this book are fictitious, and any resemblance to actual persons, living or dead, is purely coincidental.

AVON BOOKS
A division of
The Hearst Corporation
959 Eighth Avenue
New York, New York 10019

Copyright © 1969 by Lois Duncan Arquette.
Published by arrangement with Doubleday & Company, Inc.
Library of Congress Catalog Card Number: 69-11006.
ISBN: 0-380-50229-1

First Camelot Printing, January, 1971
First Avon Printing, June, 1980
Second Printing

Printed in the U.S.A.

For Kerry Elizabeth

One

The boys had been gone for three days before the police were informed, and then Mr. Drayfus was apologetic.

"It's probably ridiculous to be concerned," he admitted. "We didn't even expect them until last night, and all sorts of things can happen to slow you down when you're hiking. It's just that ever since that storm Saturday my wife has been worried, and then last night, when Larry didn't turn up, and with still no word this morning . . ."

"That rain Saturday messed up a lot of camping expeditions." The sergeant at the desk picked up a pencil and began to make notations. "When did you say they left, Mr. Drayfus? Friday evening?"

"In the afternoon, right after school. They had all the equipment assembled the night before, so they were ready to take right off. The plan was that they would get back last night in time for dinner. With school this morning, they wanted to get a good night's sleep."

The sergeant made a quick note. "And what age are the boys?"

"My son, Larry—Lawrence, Jr.—is seventeen. The other boy, Dan Cotwell, is a year or so older. I believe he's to start classes at the university in the fall." Mr. Drayfus hesitated, frowning slightly. "Larry hasn't done much camping. He's never been exactly the type. But Dan has. We figured he'd know how to deal with things in any emergency."

"I'll take their descriptions and phone the ranger station to keep an eye out for them." The sergeant smiled reassuringly at the man across the desk from him. "I wouldn't be too worried, Mr. Drayfus. This kind of thing happens all the time. There are plenty of trails in the Mogollons, and it's easy to take a wrong turn or get slowed down by a twisted ankle or something. Teenage boys are a hardy breed. They'll probably come wandering in today sometime."

"I'm sure you're right. I'm not really worried." Lawrence Drayfus returned the smile. "It's more my wife. You know how women are when it comes to the kids. They never believe they're able to take care of themselves."

"I know, all right. I'm married myself," the sergeant said comfortably. "Your wife's not the only mother who's upset this weekend. There's one young newlywed couple up there on a camping honeymoon. They were supposed to have got back last night also, and both sets of parents are having fits about them."

"I'm sure the boys will make it home by tonight," Mr. Drayfus said. "But, if they're not . . ."

"You give me a call," the sergeant told him. "If they're still missing in the morning, we'll start a concentrated search."

That was Monday.

By Wednesday, no one was being casual. Every newspaper in the state carried photographs of Lawrence Drayfus, Jr., and Daniel Cotwell.

At the shrill sound of the telephone, Joan Drayfus dropped the magazine she had been trying to read and crossed the room in quick steps to lift the receiver. It was the eighth time it had rung that morning, but repetition had not dimmed the combination of hope and fear that rose within her as she said, "Hello, Drayfus residence."

"Joan?" The voice was light and familiar. "It's Anne. I'm calling between classes. I just wanted to see if there was any news."

"No, nothing. Not yet." Joan drew a deep breath as her heart steadied into a more normal rhythm. She glanced across the room at her mother, who at the first ring, had come hurrying down the hall, and shook her head.

"There's nothing," she said again, both to the woman in the doorway and to the girl at the other end of the line. "We're just waiting."

"I bet you're going crazy," Anne said sympathetically. "Everybody at school is talking about it. The principal has excused most of the junior and senior boys to join the search party."

"I know. Dad phoned about an hour ago. He says there are more than a hundred volunteers out there. He feels terrible because he can't do any climbing himself because of his heart." She tried to make her tone bright. "Those newlyweds who were missing got home safely. What happened to them was that they couldn't find their car. They finally ended up hiking all the way back down to the highway."

"Maybe something like that happened to Dan and Larry," Anne said hopefully. "Well, we're all pulling for you. Give my love to your folks."

"I will, Anne. And thanks for calling." Joan replaced the receiver on the hook and turned to her mother. "That was Anne Tonjes. She sends her love."

"That's nice of her. Larry must have a lot of friends. There have been so many calls." Mrs. Drayfus left her place in the doorway and came into the room to sink down wearily into the closest armchair. "That phone hasn't stopped ringing since breakfast."

"Can't you lie down for a while, Mother?" Joan asked with concern. "I'm right here to get the telephone. You know I'll call you the minute there's anything to report."

"I know, dear. I wish I *could* rest. I can't turn my mind off. I keep thinking of poor little Larry, up there in the mountains somewhere . . . maybe hurt . . ."

"I can't believe that anything too terrible has happened to them," Joan said reassuringly. "Dan has been camping in those mountains for years. He's not the kind to take risks, and both of the boys are strong and healthy."

"Larry's no athlete," Mrs. Drayfus reminded her. "He's not a football hero like Dan."

"No, but he's wiry," Joan said. "He's able to take care of himself. You like to think he's delicate, Mother, but he isn't really." She went over to her mother and reached across the back of the chair to place her hands on the slumped shoulders. "Please, try to lie down for just a little while. I'm sure you didn't sleep at all last night. Can't you take one of those sedatives Dr. Cohn left for you?"

"I suppose so. I guess I'm afraid of blacking myself out. What if a call should come—*the* call—and I can't function? What if they do find them and Larry needs me?"

"You'll be of a lot more value to him if you're rested and in good condition," Joan said firmly. Even to her own ears she sounded more like the mother than the daughter.

It was with relief that she saw her mother nod her head.

"You're right, Joan, I know. But, you will call me, won't you, if there's anything? You promise? Even if I'm sleeping?"

"The very minute there's word at all," Joan assured her.

She went with her mother into the downstairs bedroom, turning down the spread, cocking the blinds against the morning light. The bottle of pills the doctor had left was on the bedside table, and she shook one out into her mother's hand and went into the bathroom for a glass of water.

"I'll call you," she promised again, and returned to the living room, as exhausted as though she herself had been climbing all night with the crew of rescuers.

Taking the seat she had left when she rose to answer the telephone, she did not attempt to pick up her magazine. Instead, she sat quietly, staring out the picture window, across the lawn, still brown from the winter cold. At the corner of the house her mother's beloved roses were beginning to bud, and beyond them the first green leaves were uncurling on the naked branches of the poplar trees. Farther still, rising to the north and west in craggy peaks, were the Mogollon Mountains.

The mountains she could see were the beginning of the range that led into the Gila Wilderness. Larry's up there now, Joan told herself, and—Dan. She focused her eyes on the distant peaks, the lower slopes softened by the morning sun. From this distance they looked so safe, so simple and familiar. There were well-traveled hiking trails and well-worn picnic areas where noisy families roasted hot dogs and gathered piñon nuts and pine cones. It didn't seem possible that people could actually get lost there, and yet, she knew, people did. The honeymooners, for instance, who had not even been able to find their automobile, and they had been on the lower slopes. Beyond these slopes was the real wilderness, some of it still unexplored, where cliffs dropped off to valleys and melting snow turned trickling streams to rushing rivers.

She had commented to her mother that the boys were strong, and it was true. Dan was six foot two, broad-shouldered and husky, with the trained muscles and stamina of a high school athlete. Larry, for all his slight appearance, had an agile, sure-footed toughness. But anyone could lose his footing in a rainstorm. Wet rocks were slippery, and if one fell and the other leaned off balance to grab him . . .

I won't think this way, Joan told herself grimly. I won't let myself. They're all right, both of them. They *have* to be!

They have to be, she repeated, and her heart seemed to fly out of her chest as the telephone jangled shrilly behind her. By the time she had reached it and had said, "Oh, Mr. Martin. No . . . no, there's no news. No, we haven't heard anything," she realized that her knees were folding beneath her.

Her brother and Dan Cotwell were *not* all right. If they were, they would have come home.

Frank Cotwell stepped out into a sudden clearing and found himself at the top of the world.

The rock on which he stood was bare and flat, cut off cleanly in front like a lookout post, from which the rocky, tree-speckled slopes fell away on three sides, giving a startling view of the river below. Even at this distance he could see the strength of the current sweeping around the jagged edges of rocks, curling out from the shore in a rim of white foam.

Good Lord, he thought, what if they were stumbling along in the rain and stepped off here!

For a moment he stood, too stunned by the horrible picture to look farther. Then, slowly, against his will, he moved to the edge of the rock and peered over into the canyon directly beneath.

For a long moment he stood, gazing downward at the boulders and long-armed bushes that would have broken the course of a falling body before it reached the bank of the river. Then, with a breath of relief that was almost a sob, he raised his eyes and began combing the slopes of the distant hills.

They had been out since before daybreak, and in late April, dawn came early in the mountains. Frank, at sixteen, had the same husky build as his older brother; he had done a lot of hiking and did not normally tire easily. He had left the rest of his search group resting while he made the climb to this lookout point. It was, he knew, the strain of worry that filled him now with such staggering weariness.

It was simply not possible that Dan could be well and uninjured and not have returned home by this time. He was too good a woodsman to have become lost in mountains he had tramped through since childhood. Dan had a fine sense of direction and always carried a compass with him; he never took chances, and in desperation he could always have scaled one of the higher peaks and, gazing out to the south, oriented himself with the sight of the city.

"Only fools get lost," Frank could remember his telling him once. It was back when the papers were full of some Boy Scout troop that had reversed itself and gone the wrong way on an outing along the edge of the Wilderness Area. "There isn't any excuse for it. It's unnecessary. Fools get lost, and fools shouldn't hike."

It was a comfort to think about Dan, solid and sensible, his eyes warm with amusement, a sprinkling of freckles lightening the lines of his square-jawed face. Dan could handle emergencies, no matter what they were. Of course, *Larry* . . .

He stiffened instinctively when he thought of Larry. Frank did not like Larry Drayfus. It was an innate dislike, based upon nothing concrete. There had never been any unpleasantness between them. There was simply a nothingness—a complete lack of empathy—which blocked any communication.

"I don't know what you want to hang around with him for," Frank had said once. "He's a cold fish. He doesn't have any friends. Heck, he doesn't even care enough about anything to make any enemies!"

"That's nothing to hold against him," Dan said in amusement. "He's a nice enough kid, even if he does keep to himself a lot. Everybody doesn't josh around like we do, you know. Besides, he comes from a swell family. You know there's got to be good stuff in him."

"Oh, come off it," Frank said irritably. "It's not Larry you go over there to see, and you know it. It's that sister of his. If she weren't there, you'd never pick Larry Drayfus to buddy around with."

"Well, you might have something there." Dan had grinned suddenly. "Joan Drayfus is a whole different person from her brother, I'll have to admit."

"Well, I don't see that either. She's no glamor girl in my book. She's too big! My gosh, Dan, she's almost as tall as you are!"

14

"Now, hold on there, little brother." The grin faded. To Frank's astonishment, all the teasing levity had vanished from his brother's voice. "I don't want to hear any slam stuff about Joanie. She's one of the nicest girls in this town. You don't have anything to judge by. You've never even dated a girl. I bet you've never even talked to one except to ask what the homework assignment is."

"For Pete's sake, Dan!" Frank had been stunned by the outburst. "All I said was that she's big! She *is*, too. You don't have to get your back up—I wasn't slamming her!"

"Well, I like her big," Dan had said shortly and clamped his mouth shut against further discussion.

It was then that Frank had realized, with a strange twinge, the depth of his brother's feelings for this tall, plain girl, whom he himself had, until now, regarded as only another in Dan's large collection of girl friends. Dan was attractive to girls and had always had a string of them at his casual command, and they had furnished a lot of joking dinner table conversation. The Cotwells were a congenial, noisy clan and, for as long as he could remember, the brothers—he and Dan and young Eddie, now twelve—had scuffled and argued and kidded each other with complete freedom. It was a closed thing, a family thing; no outsider could break into it. Among themselves there was no subject too sacred to be hashed over and laughed about.

Until now.

Now, suddenly, he could see by his brother's face, by the darkening of the blue eyes and the tight, closed set of the stubborn mouth, that the subject of Joan Drayfus, of any of the Drayfus family, for that matter, was off limits.

It was because of this that he had not said anything when Dan had announced that he was going camping with Larry.

"We're not going to try to go far," he had said. "Just kind of stretch our legs after being cooped up all winter. Larry's never done much hiking, so I don't imagine he'll be ready for too long a—hey, who the devil's been using this sleeping bag?"

"I think that's the one Eddie took last fall on that Scout pack trip." Frank stood watching him, hands in pockets.

"He must have slept with his boots on. My gosh, I'll never get all the mud out of here!" Dan gave a grunt of disgust, and then, glancing up, caught something in his brother's face that Frank had not meant him to see there.

"Say, Frankie," he said slowly, "you don't *mind* my taking off like this, do you? I mean, with Larry? He suggested it—he's never been up before, and his dad won't let him try it without somebody along who's had some experience—and I didn't really think about your minding. I know you and I usually go up together for the first campout of the year."

"Heck, why should I care?" Frank made his voice brisk. "There's the whole summer still ahead."

"I know, but—say, why don't you come with us? We can use another old hand. If Larry folds up, like I'm afraid he will, we may have to drag him piggyback all the way home."

"I'll leave you that jolly experience." Frank greeted the invitation with a shrug. "I've got other fish to fry. Besides"—suddenly he could control himself no longer; from long habit, his real feelings burst forth—"I can't see wasting a weekend on a punk like Drayfus. Sister

16

or no sister, the guy's not worth the effort. Wasn't he one of the kids at that party at the Brownings' last month, when the cops raided and found marijuana and stuff?"

"Don't believe everything you hear," Dan said shortly. "People like to talk. I've never seen Larry Drayfus take a beer or smoke a cigarette. If he was at that party, you can be darned sure he didn't know there was anything going on there. Besides, from what I hear, there *wasn't* anything going on. If there was dope of any kind there, it hadn't even been opened."

"Because the police got there before anybody had had a chance to open it," Frank began.

"Oh, can it." Dan turned back to the bedroll. "Go dig up that kid brother of ours and tell him to get here on the double, will you? He's going to spend the evening scraping mud out of this thing."

Remembering the conversation, Frank ground his nails into the palms of his hands.

I could have gone, he thought. I could have gone with him. He asked me; he wanted me. And I wanted to go. If I hadn't been so darned stubborn, I would have gone; I'd be with him now. Whatever has happened, I'd be there to help him.

Below him and to the right, a flash of color showed between the trees. In an instant, Frank was rigid with concentration. It was red. Dan hadn't been wearing red. But, perhaps Larry . . .

"Hello!" The cry tore from his throat. "Hello, down there!"

"Is that you, Frank?" The voice that shouted back was deep and familiar, but it was not Dan's voice. Not Larry's.

For a moment Frank thought he would cry with disappointment. Then he braced himself and called back to the approaching figure, now seen clearly through a break in the trees.

"I'm here, Dad! Up here on the bluff! I still haven't seen any trace of them!"

It snowed on Saturday. It was a thin snow; in the city it melted almost before it touched the ground. In the mountains it clung for a few hours to the peaks, giving them a strange, soft radiance when viewed from the valley below.

"He'll be cold," Mrs. Drayfus said. "He'll freeze, up there in a snowstorm."

"It's not a storm," Mr. Drayfus told her gently. "It's one of those freak spring snows. It will be gone before noon."

It was. In the afternoon the peaks stood bare again and the gray skies cleared.

At the Cotwell house, Mrs. Cotwell put through a load of washing and baked a pie. She washed and waxed the kitchen floor and scrubbed out the cabinets in the pantry.

"It's easier when I keep busy," she told the neighbors who flowed in and out of the small house in a steady stream. "I can't just sit here. I'd be up there on the mountain too if Ed would let me. He says women would just be in the way up there."

She gestured toward the pie. "It's lemon. Danny's favorite. They'll bring him home tonight. I just know they will. I have a feeling."

Mr. Drayfus got home a little after dusk. His wife and daughter met him at the door.

"The snow wasn't anything," he said. "Just a few flakes. We did have a little excitement though. One of the high school kids who was helping with the search took a tumble and broke his wrist. I drove him into town to the hospital. Figured I was about the most useless member of the party and could be spared the easiest, not being able to climb or anything."

"Larry?" His wife made the name a question.

"There's still tomorrow. Things look good for tomorrow. They're going to make a big thing out of it. They have two hundred volunteers lined up."

The Cotwell men arrived home an hour later. Mrs. Cotwell had the dinner table set with five places.

She said, "Eddie, you're limping!"

"It's nothing. Just a blister opened on my heel." Her youngest son was built like the others, tall and freckled, but his face still had the soft lines of childhood. Beneath the layers of dirt, it was pale and tired.

"I'll get washed," he said.

Her eyes moved to her husband and beyond him.

"Where's Frank?" she asked.

"He's coming. He's driving Dan's car back. The police jumped some wires and got it started. It was parked at the foot of the lower trail. Since the honeymoon couple had their Volkswagen stolen from the same general area, they thought it would be better if we brought it home."

"You're not telling me something." She knew him too well. She could see it behind his eyes. "They found them, didn't they? They're . . ."

"No. No, Emily, no." He shook his head violently. "All they found was a canteen. Dan's canteen. Eddie recognized it. It had a piece of tape up around the top of it."

"Where was it?" Mrs. Cotwell asked.

He could not lie to her. "Down by the river. On the bank. Tomorrow they're going to begin dragging."

Beyond him, through the open door, they could see a set of headlights turning into the driveway. Tires ground on gravel. Frank was parking it in its usual place off the edge of the drive under the elm tree.

The sound of the familiar motor roared and then fell quiet.

"Oh, dear God," Mrs. Cotwell said softly. She raised her hands to her face and, for the first time in the long week, began to cry.

Two

It was a dry spring. The warm winds of May were heavy and pink with dust from the mesas. They whipped, thick and blinding, across lawns and sent tumbleweeds whirling along the gutters and tore the first rosebuds from the bushes in the Drayfus yard.

Joan closed the windows against them and laid damp towels along the cracks beneath the doorways, and still the dust seeped into the house, dimming the rooms and settling in thick layers upon the furniture and window sills.

Outside, the dust filtered the light of the sun, bathing the world in an eerie rose-colored glow, completely obliterating the view of the mountains.

"I'm glad," Mrs. Drayfus said. "I hate them. I can't stand to look at them, great murderous things. They're like vultures, hanging there over us, waiting to snatch our children up and—and devour them."

Her voice was shrill and tight. As she had so many times in the past weeks, Joan saw her father turn toward his wife with a quick, worried glance.

"I wish you wouldn't say things like that, Margaret. They make you sound so . . . so . . ."

"What? Bitter? Heartsick? Don't I have a right to be?"

21

"Of course." He drew a long breath. "I'm heartsick too, dear. It's not just you alone. And Joan—Larry's her only brother. Still, we can't let ourselves become consumed by bitterness."

"That's easy enough for you to say," Mrs. Drayfus said. "You don't feel the way I do. If you did, you would never have let them call off the search!"

"It had to end sometime," he said patiently. "You can't keep men away from their jobs, boys out of school, indefinitely. It was as thorough as it could be. I feel sure that if Larry were there to be found, they would have found him."

"You didn't really love Larry!" Mrs. Drayfus said accusingly. "Not the way I did! You pretend you did now that he's gone, but when he was here you made his life miserable! You accused him, condemned him—"

"Margaret, that's not so!" Lawrence Drayfus exclaimed in astonishment. "Larry was my son! I loved him dearly! I never condemned him for anything!"

"You were going to send him away next fall! Against his wishes, even though he begged and begged you not to! Even though *I* begged you! All the way to Roswell to that awful military school!"

"That school in Roswell is the best in the state. It would have been the best thing in the world for Larry. He was getting out of control, Margaret—running around with the wrong crowd, getting involved in things he shouldn't. For his own good, he needed to spend his senior year somewhere where he would get direction and discipline."

"He didn't need discipline—just understanding! Love and understanding! You never tried to get really close to Larry! He was a sensitive boy, high-strung, emo-

22

tional, even though he didn't show it on the outside! You can't take a boy like that and cram him into a mold like a million other boys!"

Her voice was becoming shriller. Joan got up quickly and crossed to her and put her arm around her.

"Please, Mommy." She spoke the name softly, the old name from childhood. "You mustn't get so upset. We all loved Larry, each of us in our own way. You can't keep going over and over it like this. You'll make yourself sick."

"He should never have gone on that camping trip," Margaret Drayfus said in a lower voice. "It was ridiculous. I said so, right from the start. Larry isn't the kind of boy to go climbing up and down dirty rocks. It was that Cotwell boy—he talked him into it—"

"Mother, you're wrong!" Joan said in automatic defense. "Really, it was Larry who suggested the camping weekend. He asked Dan to go. I heard him. He wanted to get out because . . ."

The sentence trailed off.

"Because, why?" her mother asked sharply.

"Just because"—Joan cast a compassionate glance at her father's set face—"because he—he thought it would be fun."

It was not the complete truth, but the lie, if it could be termed such, was a kind one. She could not increase the grief in her father's eyes by quoting the words as they had actually been spoken.

Reluctantly, her mind plunged back to that day, now almost three weeks past, when she and Dan had been doing their homework together at the kitchen table.

Larry had strolled in and stood watching them a moment. Then, without preamble, he said, "Dan, let's go camping this weekend."

"Camping?" Dan had glanced up in surprise. "Hey, what's got into you? You've never been interested in that sort of thing."

"Well, there's always a first time."

There had been something in his voice that made Joan raise her eyes quickly from her book. She and Larry had never been close, it was true. In looks, in temperament, in personality, it would have been difficult to have found two more opposite people. Still, he was her brother, she loved him and had grown up with him, and she felt a sudden strange awareness that something was not exactly as it should be.

"Come clean, Larry," she said lightly. "What's behind this violent yen for the great out-of-doors? It's never affected you before."

"Since when does a guy have to give reasons every time he wants to commune with nature?" Larry's green eyes were wide with innocent bewilderment. He held the pose for a long moment, and then, quickly, deserted it.

"Okay, Miss Bloodhound, if you must know. Dad's got me grounded this weekend. Since that party at Brownings', he's cracked down, but hard. I can't use the car. I have to be in the house at nine o'clock. I have to tell him every time I want to step out long enough to go to a movie. He may not be able to send me off to military school until next fall, but he's damned well going to start things off right by making his own little military school right here at home."

"What makes you think he's going to let you take off for a camping weekend?" Joan asked.

"The way I figure it, it's the only kind of outing he *will* let down the bars for. He's always been after me to get out and rough around like he did at my age. And he thinks Dan's the greatest—a real good influence on me. With Dan as my bodyguard, he's bound to say yes."

Suddenly his face broke into a grin of such irresistible impishness that Joan found herself smiling back despite herself.

"Come on, Dan, be a sport! Don't leave me here to climb the walls all weekend!"

"Go ahead, Dan, and give in," Joan said in amusement. "You've been chafing at the bit to get up into the mountains, and you know it."

"Well, if you don't mind taking a rain check on our movie date." It had not taken much persuasion; she had known that it wouldn't.

"Knowing the State Theater, that picture will still be showing six months from now," Joan said. "Besides, with exams coming up next month and two book reports due, I shouldn't be hopping off to the movies anyway."

It had all been arranged so easily. Mr. Drayfus had been pleased at Larry's unusual burst of enthusiasm for an out-of-doors weekend.

"It will be good for him," he had said.

Mrs. Drayfus, it was true, had voiced hesitation, but not a great deal. It was only in afterthought that it reappeared to her as real objection.

"You'll probably come home exhausted," she had said. "For goodness sake, take enough warm clothing. I hear it's still pretty cold up in the mountains at night in April."

Later, when she had passed her brother in the hall, Joan had surprised herself by reaching out a hand to detain him.

"Larry . . . are you sure . . ." She hesitated, uncertain of exactly what she was disturbed about.

"Sure of what?" he had asked her blankly.

"That getting away—not having to sit around here all weekend—is *really* the reason you want Dan to go camping with you?"

"What other reason could there be?" He smiled at her, the quick, sweet smile that, together with the soft blond hair, tumbled childlike over his forehead, made him look about twelve years old.

"None, I guess." She wondered if she looked as sheepish as she felt. "Have fun."

The smile faded. "I don't really expect to," Larry had said, "but it will be better than being shut up here with Dad standing over me like a prison warden."

Now, gazing at her parents' weary faces, Joan could see no reason for repeating the conversation. They were grieved enough without her dredging up bitter words to add to their pain. Besides, Larry had not really meant them; he was angry, flaring up defiantly the way teenage boys did when their first tries at independence were stepped upon. Her father would be hurt to the quick to know that these were the last words his son had spoken about him, and her mother looked as though one more ounce of pressure of any kind might be more than she could handle.

Mrs. Drayfus was a small woman, delicately pretty and highly sensitive. It was from her that Larry had come by his looks; both mother and son were slender and small-boned with fair skin and hair.

Joan, on the other hand, resembled her father, tall and hardy with a down-to-earth sensibility.

"It isn't fair!" she had cried once, despairingly, back in the early days of grade school. "It isn't fair for Larry to be pretty when I'm the girl!"

"You're pretty too, Joanie," her father had said soothingly. "You're a different kind of pretty. Everybody can't be the same."

"But Larry's kind of looks are what people like!" Joan had insisted.

"That's not so." Her father had regarded her gravely out of kind gray eyes, set beneath the heavy brows that were so much like her own. "Everybody has his own idea of what is beautiful."

She had carried those words with her for many years, not really believing them, but using them for comfort when times were difficult, when crowd activities began to give way to dating ones and schoolmates started to fall into pairs. It was not that she didn't have dates of her own. She was well liked by boys and girls alike, and she seldom sat home from a party. But the dates she had were casual, friendly ones, uncolored by romance, and she was painfully aware of the fact that the boys who invited her had usually been turned down by one or two other girls first.

And then—there was Dan. In the beginning, she knew, she had been a second-choice date for him, too. She had not really minded that; it was something to be escorted to a dance by Dan Cotwell, no matter how it happened. The startling thing was that he had called her again the next weekend. And again after that. It had gone on like that, increasing slowly, unbelievably, becoming deeper, drawing forth more of each of them, until one incredible day she had looked into his eyes and seen herself reflected there. And she had been beautiful.

From then on, it no longer mattered that she was different from Larry. He was himself, just as she was Joan; they were what they were, and that was that. She was even able to smile when she saw the softening of her mother's face when she looked at her son.

That's just the way mothers are, she told herself. Someday I'll have a son of my own, and I'll probably be just the same way about him.

She was not ready yet to admit to herself that the son in her dreams had the blue eyes and cinnamon hair of Dan Cotwell.

Now, before the real and consuming pain in her mother's eyes, her own heart filled with an echoing agony. Larry had been her brother, and Dan—she would not let herself think of Dan. She pressed him from her mind, knowing that if she let herself picture him her control would break. This could not happen. Not yet. Not at this crucial sharp-edged time when her parents needed her so desperately.

Strange as it seemed, quite suddenly their positions seemed to have reversed. It was she who was the oldest, the strongest. It was Joan who took the phone calls, who planned the meals, who saw to it that the household continued in its routine course.

"Mother," she said now, "don't you want to lie down for a little before dinner?"

"Dinner?" Her mother regarded her blankly.

"I picked up a steak at the market. I thought that would be quick and easy."

"Oh. Oh—yes, dear. All right." Mrs. Drayfus got up slowly. The very obedience, the childlike acceptance of direction, was in its way more frightening than the previous irrational spurt of anger.

Afternoon gave way to evening. Still the wind continued. The house was stuffy, with its windows closed against the sweeping dust.

Joan broiled the steak and served it with a salad, knowing as she did so that most of it would remain untouched. After the token meal, her father turned on the television set in the den. Mrs. Drayfus sat before it, staring at the screen, watching the lifelike shadows flickering, singing, laughing in their own unreal world.

Normally she did not watch television at all. "Silly old one-eyed monster," she called it, preferring to read or chat or play bridge with friends. Now television seemed to fill a great need in her existence. She let it fill her evenings, blanking her mind, occupying her eyes and her senses.

Joan regarded her worriedly.

Mr. Drayfus helped his daughter clear the table.

"I talked to the doctor about your mother," he said in a low voice when they stood together in the kitchen. "He says she is in a kind of shock. Her mind, her heart, everything in her is refusing to accept what has happened. It's this business of not knowing—the waiting, the uncertainty. It will be better when . . ."

He stopped.

"When what? Joan asked, bracing herself.

"When"—her father's voice was flat with agony— "when the river goes down and they're able to find the bodies."

"You can't mean that!" Joan, in her horror, could hardly scrape out the words.

"I do mean it," Mr. Drayfus said. "It will be better to have the final proof, to have it over and finished, to

29

know. There's a place for hope, but after this long—well, there's a point for it to end also. Your mother will be able to accept the loss if it's final and inevitable. At least, I hope she will."

"Oh, Dad!" Joan's eyes were dim with tears. "The whole thing is so . . . so . . ."

The telephone rang.

"Get it, will you, Joan?" Mr. Drayfus said. "If it's for your mother, just say she's resting."

"All right." Joan went into the living room and lifted the receiver. "Hello. Drayfus residence."

"Is this Mrs. Drayfus?" The voice was a man's, smoothly formal, unfamiliar.

"Mrs. Drayfus is resting right now," Joan said. "This is her daughter. May I help you?"

"Well, maybe you can," the man said. "It's about your brother. I read in the paper about the tragedy. How he was drowned up in the Mogollons. A sad thing, a terrible thing. You have my sympathy."

"Thank you," Joan said. She paused and then asked, "Who is this? Were you a friend of Larry's?"

"Well, sort of. Not exactly. You might say I'm a—a business associate." The voice changed as the veil of formal sympathy dropped from it. "As a matter of fact, Larry's death affects me in a business way. He died with some money—*my* money—in his possession. I thought I'd call and see about collecting it."

"Larry had money of yours?" Joan repeated the words in astonishment.

"I'm afraid he did. I'm sure he intended to repay it immediately, but under the circumstances . . ." He did not continue.

"I don't understand," Joan said. "I didn't know Larry was involved in any business. Exactly how much money did he owe you?"

"Quite a bit," the man's cool voice told her. "Like, would you believe, upwards of two thousand dollars?"

Three

Finals were held the last week in May. Frank Cotwell knew before he took them that he would do poorly. He had been out of school for a week during the time he was with the search party, and when he did at last return to class it was impossible for him to keep his mind on studying. He could, he found, sit for hours, staring at an open book, without completing a page. The words swam before his eyes, blurred and meaningless, while his mind went back again and again, reliving that last day when Dan had tossed his pack into the back seat of his car and said, "Sure you won't change your mind?"

"Sure, thanks."

In that last instant, Frank had almost relented. The weekend stretched ahead of him, unplanned and empty. The house was always lifeless when Dan wasn't in it. It was crazy really because there were still four of them there to fill it. There was still the same amount of noise and busyness, but there was something about the presence of Dan that seemed to solidify the family, to give each member his place. It was hard to put your finger on it, but whatever it was, it was there.

Then, just as he was reconsidering, Larry Drayfus had turned in the front seat and glanced back at him.

"Sure, Frank," he had said. "Come on along."

The words had been right, but there had been something—some quick flash of expression, a darkening of the green eyes—that had let Frank know with no room for doubt that the words held no meaning. Larry did not want him.

And Dan—well, Dan was being nice. Maybe he felt a little guilty about taking Larry along on what was usually kind of an occasion, the first overnight of the season.

"Thanks, but no thanks," Frank had said shortly, and turned and went into the house.

Where was Dan now? While he sat at the school desk, staring at the examination questions, his mind went without him, trudging along footpaths, over boulders, crossing rivers, gazing down through trees into crevices. Somewhere, somewhere, Dan Cotwell existed still. People did not just vanish from the face of the earth. Alive or dead, Dan was somewhere. Dead? It was an incredible word to attach to someone as alert, as alive, as his brother. Everything within him fought against acceptance, and yet . . .

It had been a full month now. The sunlight sliding through the window to fall golden across the desk was heavy and warm, not the thin pale sun of April. At home, outside the window of the bedroom he shared with Eddie, birds were already nesting in the branches of the elm tree. Up and down the street, people were fertilizing their lawns and sprinklers were throwing high bright rainbows against the sky, and spring was deepening into the edge of summer.

A whole month gone—and no word—no sign.

"Five minutes," Miss Fitzgerald said warningly.

With an effort, Frank forced his mind to focus on the

questions before him. *Silas Marner—Enoch Arden;*
he had read them. Sometime during the last semester
he had read and digested them, but it seemed so long
ago. The names, the events—there seemed no importance to them; they were fictional characters from a
story book land of unreality.

One of them had gone away on a voyage and not
returned. Which one was it? And he *had* eventually,
hadn't he? Years and years later? And his wife had
remarried, had made a life with someone else in the
meantime?

Abruptly, his mind flashed to Joan Drayfus. It was
not a flight he had willed it to take. He had never paid
much attention to the girls his brother dated, and Joan
was certainly one of the least impressive of them. In
his own opinion, girls should be little and dainty, like
Marcie Summers, for instance, who was in his math
class, and whom he had never managed to speak to, but
whom he had watched all year, tossing her long blond
hair back over her slim shoulders and biting delicately
at the end of her pencil.

Joan's lack of prettiness, while it should reasonably
have made him more at ease with her, had never been
enough to overcome his nervous awareness that she was
a girl. In the maleness of the Cotwell household, a girl
was like a creature from another planet. Dan had
brought her over to the house a few times for one reason or another, to study or to watch television, and
once she had come for dinner. She hadn't talked much,
as Frank recalled; she had sat there quietly, eating his
mother's savory pot roast, turning every once in a while
to smile at Dan, seemingly a little awed by the noise
and confusion of the family dinner table. Her presence
had put things into a different perspective, and sud-

denly Frank himself had seen things as loud and riotous. He had become momentarily embarrassed, and then, ashamed of his reaction, had plunged into the conversation more violently than ever.

Joan was just another girl, he assured himself. Dan would drop her eventually, just as he had dropped a dozen other girls in the past. They were not going steady, at least not officially. But it *had* been a long time since he could remember Dan's dating anyone else. They certainly spent a lot of time together. On week nights they studied. On weekends they were always off somewhere doing something, a party or a movie or bowling or—gosh, he didn't know exactly what all they did do when they were together.

"They kiss each other!" Eddie had declared once. "Mush—sqush—all that kind of stuff, like in the movies! Big brother's a regular Rock Hudson!"

"You're nuts," Frank had said, surprised at the violence of his own reaction.

"Then why does he get lipstick all over his handkerchiefs? I saw one in the laundry basket."

"Well, cripes, maybe he lent it to her or something."

Of course, Dan *did* kiss her. Even though it gave him an odd feeling to think about it, Frank had to acknowledge the fact squarely. His brother was eighteen years old and had been dating girls since he was much younger than Frank was now. He had been going with Joan Drayfus for over a year now; they had started dating a year ago Christmas, to be exact. He could remember because it was at a formal. Dan had asked Anne Tonjes, but she had already had a date with somebody, and then he had called another girl, and finally he had called Anne's friend Joan.

"It's what I get for waiting so long," he had said lightly.

At that time, he had said such things. He had not pretended then that Joan was pretty or exciting or somebody to be cherished. She had been, quite simply, a pleasant, not particularly attractive girl who was usually free for a date when you were late getting your bid in and the more popular girls were already taken.

Where had it changed? Frank was not sure. He had not been interested enough to notice. Still, it had happened. It was no light feeling that had brought the cold steel into his brother's eyes and the quick outburst that night before the camping trip:

"I don't want to hear any slam stuff about Joanie!"

Miss Fitzgerald's voice broke into his consciousness.

"Time! Will you pass your papers to the front, please?"

Well, that's an F, Frank thought with resignation.

Six weeks ago the thought of flunking a final would have filled him with horror. Now, it hardly seemed to matter. What was a grade but a mark on a sheet of paper? Dan had been an all-A student. He had won a scholarship to the university for the coming fall. Did it matter now?

Bitterly, Frank handed his paper forward along with the others and got to his feet to join the line of students filing out of the classroom.

Outside in the hall, Roger Ruvolo and a couple of the other fellows were waiting for him.

"That wasn't as bad as I expected," Roger said, falling into step beside him. "That's my last final. What'll we do to celebrate?"

"I promised Mom I'd get the lawn fertilized," Frank said.

Without looking he could feel the exchange of glances that passed across him.

"Come on, Frankie." Scott Kimball's voice was a little too bright to be casual. "You've got the whole rest of the day for that. Heck, you've got the whole rest of the summer! The public pool opened last weekend. Why don't we go out there and get cooled off?"

"Great idea," Roger said enthusiastically. "If we hurry we can make the twelve-thirty bus or—say, Frank, can't you get the Chevvy?"

"That's Dan's," Frank said shortly.

"Sure. I know that, I just thought—I mean, it's just sitting there . . ."

Roger's voice faded off in embarrassment.

"I told you, I've got to get the yard done." Frank thrust his hands deep into his pants pockets. "I'll see you around."

"Sure. Yeah. See you around, Frank."

He was conscious of their eyes upon him as he broke away and turned through the east door out into the golden sunlight.

The scent of spring broke upon him, fresh and sweet. The air was light with laughter as groups of students hurried past him, giddy with release, chattering like sparrows.

Bits of conversations swirled at him from all sides:

". . . was the most unfair question I ever saw! We didn't even *study* that period of history . . ."

". . . party at Cathy Beahm's tonight. I'm going to wear my fall. Mother promised . . ."

". . . go fishing at Navajo Lake the first of June. My uncle went last weekend and he says they're biting like mad . . ."

Determinedly, Frank cut across the grass and crossed

the street. The voices, the laughter, the gay discussions of vacations and parties fell away behind him as he hurried his footsteps until he was almost running.

Dopey stuff, he thought. Dopey kid stuff. Parties meant getting dressed up and dancing; he never went to them if he could help it. Marcie would undoubtedly be at the Beahms' party. He could imagine what she would look like, all dressed up in some fluffy dress with her hair piled high on top of her head, but the thought of actually dancing with her made his stomach knot in panic. He'd step all over her. And vacations . . . well, last year the whole family had driven to the lake at Elephant Butte and it had been pretty great. They had taken a cabin for a couple of weeks, and Eddie had learned to swim, and he and Dan had rented a canoe, but this year . . . well, it was different. Just the word "vacation" was enough to cause a stab of pain. What kind of vacation could they have now, his parents and Eddie and himself, with the shadow of Dan there among them, the terrible hole gaping in the family?

He bit down hard on his lower lip to keep it from trembling. It was like this lately. Everything he heard, everything he thought carried him back to Dan and the realization of how close, how very close, they had been, and all the time he hadn't realized it, had taken it so completely for granted. . . .

"Frank?"

The girl had been walking ahead of him. He had been aware of her without seeing her, without actually raising his eyes and looking. She was alone, and she had been walking about three yards ahead, and now she had stopped and turned and was standing, waiting for him to catch up with her.

"Frank—hi."

"Oh, hi, Joan." There was no escaping it, for now he *had* caught up with her, and she had begun to walk again, beside him.

"I heard your footsteps behind me," she said. "It's funny—the sound of your footsteps. For a moment there, before I turned around, it sounded like Dan."

"Yeah. People have always said that. We walk alike. It's having long legs."

"I guess so. I mean, that sounds like a reasonable reason."

She sounded tired. Despite himself, Frank raised his eyes and turned his head to glance sideways at her. She didn't look good. Although she had never been glamorous, she had always had something—a kind of glow about her—a warm, healthy look. She didn't have that now. She had lost weight, and with her height she could not afford to. Her cheeks had a sunken look, and her eyes were shadowed, and there was a pale dullness to her skin.

She looks about the way I feel, Frank thought.

Aloud he said, "Well, school's about out." It was a stupid thing to say, but at least it broke the silence.

"Yes. Graduation is this weekend."

"That's right. I'd forgotten. You're graduating this year, aren't you?"

Dan was to have graduated too. The announcements had been ordered and they had arrived two weeks ago. The box was at home on the hall table. His mother had opened them; he was not sure just why. She hadn't addressed them though.

"Fifty announcements!" Dan had exclaimed when she ordered them. "My gosh, Mom, you'd think I was graduating from Harvard or something! This is just high school, remember?"

"When your oldest son graduates from high school, that's important enough for announcing," his mother had said firmly. "All the relatives will want announcements, and the men Dad works with."

There would have been a big group of Cotwells at the graduation exercises, that was for sure—aunts and uncles and cousins and assorted in-laws. The Cotwells always had a turnout for any family event.

Now, of course, there was no reason for attending. He had almost forgotten that Joan would be graduating.

"Anne Tonjes is valedictorian," Joan said. "She has the highest grades in the class, except for Dan's. His average was two points higher."

"You mean, Dan would have been—that?"

Joan nodded. "The principal announced it at the senior class meeting."

"Gee."

Like the scholarship, it didn't matter now, but it would be something, Frank thought, to tell his mother. It would mean something to her, the fact that Dan would have been valedictorian of his graduating class.

"Dan had the brains in the family," he said. "I'll be doing great if I ever pass this year. I know I just flunked the English exam. It's hard—I can't keep my mind on things."

"I know."

There was such understanding in her voice that he realized that she *did* know. Suddenly, he felt a deep rush of sympathy for the girl walking beside him. It transcended all previous feelings, his resentment of Joan for taking such an important place in his brother's life, his discomfort with girls in general.

With a gesture completely foreign to himself, he reached over and patted her shoulder.

The touch, light as it was, brought an unexpected reaction. Abruptly, Joan raised her hands to cover her face.

"Frank," she said in a muffled voice, "Frank, I don't know what to do."

They had reached the corner that marked the breaking point on the way to their different houses. Now, standing there on the sunny sidewalk, Frank had the frightened feeling that the girl beside him was, herself, breaking. The tight control seemed suddenly to have snapped. She stood very still, with her hands pressed to her face.

"Joan," he said uncertainly. "Please, don't. You know you can't do anything. Everybody's already done everything they can. The search was thorough. I know—I was there. They couldn't keep it going month after month. They had to call an end somewhere."

"I know. That's not what I mean." She lowered her hands. Her face was very white, but to his surprise he saw that she was not crying.

"It's something else," she said. "Frank, can I talk to you? I have to talk to somebody. I can't go to my parents, not in the state they're in now."

"Sure. Talk about anything you want to." Frank nodded at the little green island across the street. "Let's go over to the park. We can sit there for a while if you want to."

"Thanks." She tried to smile, but it looked more like a grimace, her mouth straining to turn up at the corners while her eyes remained empty.

"Come on."

He took her arm and steered her across the street without even realizing that it was the first time he had ever made such a gesture. The look on her face frightened him, and he knew somehow that it was caused by something other than grief.

When they reached the park, he led her down a path to a bench. The midday sun was warm, and the park was empty except for some children tossing a ball back and forth a distance away.

"Okay," Frank said as they sat down, "Shoot. What's happened?"

"It was a phone call." Joan brought the words out in a rush, as though in relief at finally being able to speak them. "It wasn't for me, at least, it wasn't meant to be. The man wanted to speak to Mother. I answered and told him she was resting and asked what he wanted. He—he wanted money."

"Money?" Frank did not know what he had expected her to tell him, but it was certainly not this. "Why?"

"He said Larry owed it to him. A lot of money, Frank. Two thousand dollars."

"Two thousand dollars!" Frank echoed the words incredulously. "How could Larry owe anybody that amount? Who was this guy anyway?"

"He said his name was Brown. John Brown. The way he said it, I don't think he meant for me to believe him. He said that he and Larry had been in a—a business deal together—and that Larry was holding the money. Now, with Larry—gone—he wants it paid to him."

"What kind of business deal?" Frank asked. "Larry was only seventeen, just a year older than I am. How could he be involved in business deals where he would be handling that kind of cash?"

"I don't know. Mr. Brown wouldn't say. What he inferred was that Larry's part in whatever it is wasn't quite on the up-and-up. He said he didn't want to hurt

Larry's reputation by having any publicity about it if he could help it. All he wanted was for the money to be located and turned over to him."

"What did your parents say?" Frank asked. "You did tell them about it, didn't you?"

"I *couldn't,*" Joan said. "That's the whole thing, Frank—my parents mustn't know about this. They're not well, either one of them. My father has a bad heart—he had a slight attack a year ago—and he's not supposed to be under pressure of any kind. I don't know how he's managed to hold up through all that's happened these past weeks. It's a kind of miracle. And Mother—she isn't herself. Daddy calls it shock, but whatever it is, it's getting worse instead of better. Sometimes I wonder if she knows us at all, she's so wrapped up in thinking about Larry. She won't believe he's dead. She has him built up in her mind until he's some sort of angel. To have somebody come out now with accusations against him—she just couldn't handle it. I *can't* tell them."

"So what did you do?" Frank asked her. "You must have told the man something over the phone?"

"I told him not to try to talk to my parents. I said I'd take care of things."

"You!" Frank exclaimed. "My gosh, Joan, how do you plan to do that? You don't have two thousand dollars sitting around any place, do you?"

"No, but I do have *some* money," Joan said defiantly. "I've had a savings account for years now. I've done a lot of babysitting, and last summer I worked as a counselor at Girl Scout camp. I was going to use the money for clothes and extras next fall for college."

"And the rest of the money?"

"Well, I could get it somehow. At least, I could try.

Now, with Dan gone . . ." Her voice came with a choking sound. "College doesn't seem so . . . wonderful, any more. I don't really care whether I go or not. I could get a job instead and repay the money month by month. Mother and Daddy wouldn't have to know anything about it."

"You must be crazy," Frank said flatly. "You don't even know that this Mr. Brown is telling you the truth. Larry may not owe him a penny. He may not have had anything to do with him. You read about con men like that, guys who follow up every tragedy in the paper and contact the families and make claims. This business of not wanting to hurt his reputation could just be a kind of blackmail."

"I know," Joan said miserably. "Still, Larry *was* running a little wild this past year. Dad was worried enough about it to decide to send him away to school next fall. Not that Larry would ever have done anything really bad. I'm sure he wouldn't have. But he's not here to defend himself, and this man says he has proof, that Larry signed a paper, an IOU for the money."

"And you're taking him at his word?"

"Of course not. I'm not that dumb." Joan's face was beginning to take on some color now, the pink flush of anger. "I told him I'd have to see the paper. I know Larry's handwriting. Nobody could fool me about that. I'm to meet him tomorrow night. He said he'd bring it to show to me. The conversation—it all seemed to come so fast. It wasn't until after he'd hung up and I started to think about it that I realized what I'd promised, and now—Frank, I'm scared."

"You should be," Frank said shortly. "That's about the dumbest thing I've ever heard of, a girl going out alone to meet some strange man who doesn't even

44

give her his right name. Where is this meeting supposed to take place?"

"At the library. On the steps. I promised—if I don't go, he's going to get in touch with my parents. He might call while I was out and Mother might answer the phone and—Frank . . ." The anger was gone now; all that was left was desperation. "Frank, what can I do? I've promised! I have to be there!"

"Yes, I guess you do," Frank said quietly. "But you're darned sure not going to go by yourself. I'll go with you, and we'll talk to this—Mr. Brown—together."

Four

He was not sure how long he had slept, but he was awakened by the sound of the apartment door opening and closing. He kept his eyes determinedly closed, reluctant to tear himself away from the comfort of unconsciousness.

There was a long pause as the person in the doorway stood, silently. Then he heard the soft pad of rubber-soled shoes and caught the scent of suntan oil.

A voice spoke softly. "Dave?"

With a sigh, the boy on the bed opened his eyes, and the world came into being about him.

"Hi," he said.

"Have you been asleep all the time I've been gone? How are you feeling?"

"Okay, I guess. What's with you? I thought you were going job hunting?"

"I did, but no luck. I had my swimming stuff in the car, and I stopped off at the beach on my way back. It was really great. We're going to have to get a surf board. Everybody out here seems to have one."

The younger boy shoved his damp hair back from his forehead and tossed his towel over the back of a chair. He was dressed in red and blue plaid swimming shorts and a white T-shirt. His eyes were clear and green in his tanned face.

"Boy, I'm hungry. Is there anything to eat around here?"

"I think there are some apples left in that bag on the table. There was a sack of cookies somewhere around too."

Dave pulled himself to a sitting position. He felt as groggy and dragged out as though he had been toiling outside in the hot sun instead of napping the entire afternoon indoors.

"Where did you go?" he asked. "Did you look into that ad for a department store salesman? That one looked kind of promising. With a new store opening up like that, there ought to be a lot of different openings."

"I applied, but I don't think anything's going to come of it. I look too young. They acted like I still ought to be in school."

"Well, tomorrow," Dave said, "I'll take a crack at it myself. We've got to get some money coming in. This may not be much of a room, but it costs something, and so do those apples you're eating. And gas for the car. And that surf board you're so keen on buying."

"I wish you'd stop worrying. We've got enough cash to get along for a little while." The blondhaired boy had found the cookies and was preparing to make a meal of them. "You're not ready to go out and start working yet. You might keel over or something, and have a relapse."

"A relapse?" Dave laughed shortly. "That would be pretty difficult. I don't have anything to relapse to. My gosh, Lance, it's just as blank now as it was the first day we got here!"

"You're sure?" Lance regarded him critically. "You

seem better. Isn't it starting to come back to you at all? Not anything?"

"Nothing. It's like—well, like I just got born right here in this room. I remember yesterday and the day before that and—oh, I have a vague recollection of the drive west. Not much though. It's the darnedest feeling. You can't imagine."

"Don't let it panic you, Dave," Lance said sympathetically. "You were sick, real sick. You ran a very high fever for a couple of weeks there. The doctor said it wasn't unusual for this to happen, not after a bout like that. It's a wonder you lived at all."

"Maybe I ought to look up a doctor out here and get checked again," Dave said. "I don't even remember the one in New York. How long did he think it would take for me to start snapping out of this? I ought to be getting better by this time, shouldn't I?"

"You *are* better," Lance told him firmly. "A lot better. You don't know how bad you were. Heck, Dave, you're bound to be under par for a while, maybe even a long while. Your strength is starting to come back now, and your memory will too. The thing you don't want to do is push yourself too hard. Instead of going out looking for work tomorrow, you ought to go over to the beach. Get some fresh air and sunshine."

"Okay, okay. I know you're right. I'm expecting too much too fast."

Swinging his legs over the side of the bed, Dave got to his feet and crossed over to the French doors, which opened out onto the balcony. He stood there silently, gazing out at the world below.

Their room was a small one and the building old; the French doors themselves were sealed to prevent the room's occupants from stepping out onto the balcony, which, the landlord had informed them, was in need of repair. Inside the room, the chipped blue walls needed a coat of paint. The air from the one small window was set in languid motion by a large, old-fashioned fan, revolving slowly against the dingy ceiling.

The room was far indeed, from luxurious, but the view, as seen across the useless balcony, was something else entirely. The street below was lined with royal poincianas, green when they had first arrived, but now beginning to blossom out in masses of unbelievable scarlet blooms. The trees led the way in two bright trails to the end of the street where a strip of white proclaimed the sand of a public beach. Beyond that lay the water, glistening blue beneath the brighter blue of the sky. Over it all, the late afternoon sunlight fell in a golden haze.

"I guess it must be pretty different from New York," Dave said slowly.

"Different? It's a whole new world!" Lance had finished the cookies. Now he went over to the closet and selected a tan sports jacket and a pair of slacks. He carried them over to the second bed and laid them out carefully across the spread.

"I'm going down the hall to get a shower. Are there any clean towels?"

"There were, but I think you took the last one to the beach with you." Dave turned to stare at him. "You going out some place?"

"I met some guys at the beach. They're going out on the town tonight. They asked me if I wanted to go along."

" 'Out-on-the-town' costs money," Dave said. "With both of us out of work, I'd think you could take a rain check on that kind of evening."

49

"Dave, relax, won't you?" Lance regarded him with unconcealed exasperation. "I told you, we've got enough to get along. We're not going to starve tomorrow because I go out tonight. I'll pick up a job this next week. Maybe one of the guys I'm going out with tonight will steer me into one. Just stop worrying about everything!"

"Okay, I'll try."

As often happened, Dave found himself studying the younger boy's face—blond hair, green eyes, the delicate tracery of cheekbones beneath the tanned skin. A face that could not be more different from his own.

And yet, they were brothers.

He could remember Lance's face bending worriedly over him:

"Dave? Are you feeling better, Dave?"

"Who"—Dave had stared up at him groggily—"who are you?"

"I'm Lance! Don't you remember me, your brother, Lance? Dave, you've *got* to remember me!"

"Yeah . . . yeah, I guess . . ."

There *had* been something familiar; he knew the face. It did not belong to a stranger. And yet, to have this boy his brother . . .

My brother! Dave shook his head, trying to clear the dizziness, to break through the cloudy curtain that hung there. My younger brother! We must have spent a lot of years together, Lance and I. We must have ridden bikes together, played ball, helped each other in and out of scrapes. Did I help him with his homework when we were kids? I must have known him when he was a baby, when that thin face was soft and rounded. I must have been a baby myself when our mother first brought him home from the hospital. Our mother . . .

"Lance?" He spoke suddenly. "What about our mother? Where are our parents? Back in New York?"

"We don't have parents," Lance said. "They were killed, both of them. It was an automobile accident, about five years ago."

"Then, that's where that money we're living on came from?"

"Sure. They left it to us."

"Who did we live with then?" Dave asked. "Back east, I mean?"

"We didn't live with anybody. We had our own apartment."

"Just the two of us? For five years?"

"We don't have any other relatives," Lance told him. "It's just you and me, Dave—in New York or here in California. Just us. Now, if you'll let me off from the third degree for a few minutes, I want to get the salt washed off."

His smile took the edge from the words. Lance had a wonderful smile that lit up his face like sunshine.

My brother, Dave thought wonderingly. Perhaps he looks like one of our parents and I look like the other. A mother—a father—both dead. But there were years before that—years when we were a family! There was a past life, other places, other people—and I don't remember it!

Dear Lord, I don't remember any of it at all!

Five

They had been waiting on the steps for half an hour, and no one had come.

"Maybe it was a joke," Frank suggested. "There are people like that, you know, nuts who think it's funny to call people with troubles and make things worse for them. They could have got Larry's name and address from one of the newspaper articles."

"It wasn't a joke," Joan said.

She did not know why she was so certain about this. It was nothing for which she had an actual explanation. It had been something in the voice itself, in the abrupt businesslike tone that had followed the artificial offer of sympathy.

"It wasn't a joke," she said again. "Perhaps I got the time wrong."

"You wouldn't have done that."

"I could have, I suppose. I was rattled. Maybe he said tomorrow night, or last night even." She turned to face the boy beside her. "Anyway, he's not here. It's a half hour past now. If he were coming he would be here by this time."

Frank frowned thoughtfully. In the dim half-light that flowed out to them through the glass doors of the library, his resemblance to Dan was even more striking than usual. The freckles stood out in dark spots across the bridge of his nose, and beneath them his face was white and worried.

"You wouldn't have got twisted up on something as important as this."

It was true, and Joan knew it. Every word of the conversation was engraved on her memory:

"The library steps—eight o'clock—Friday."

Of course, there were branch libraries. She had assumed immediately that the one meant was the main library, because it *was* the main one, and because it was only a short bus ride from her home. Yet, there were other libraries scattered here and there about the city. Could the man, even now, be waiting at one of them, checking his watch, wondering angrily where she was and why she had not arrived as promised? Might he, in his anger, turn at last and enter the library and ask to use the telephone and try to call her? If so, one of her parents would answer.

"Hello," the smooth voice would say. "This is John Brown. I want to talk to you about your son Larry."

The mere thought of the conversation that would follow was enough to leave her feeling sick. And tonight was the worst time it could take place. That scene at the dinner table . . .

Joan shuddered, remembering.

"Whatever the reason, he's evidently not coming." She glanced again at her watch. "We can't keep on waiting. I told my folks I'd be home by nine-thirty."

"You'll make it by then. There ought to be a bus by here in a few minutes."

Frank got up stiffly from his seat on the top step, stretching his long legs to get the kinks out of them, straightening his shoulders in the way Dan used to.

"Come on, we'd better walk down to the corner."

They arrived at the bus stop just as the bus itself pulled to a halt, its doors rippling open before them. They climbed on and found seats easily; it was not a time of evening for people to be hunting for transportation. Those who were going some place for the evening had already gone, and it was not yet late enough for them to be returning. Even the youngest moviegoer stayed out through the end of the first feature.

It was far from the first time Joan had taken the bus to the library after dinner. She had mentioned it casually at the table, without a thought that there might be an objection.

She was completely unprepared for her mother's reaction:

"Why do you need to go out tonight? Now that school's out, you can go to the library any time you want during the day. It's not safe for a girl to be wandering around alone in the evening."

"For goodness sake, Mother, I used to go to the library a couple of nights a week during the school year! You never worried about it before." Joan regarded her with honest surprise. "The bus stops right down at the end of our block and again at the corner by the library."

"You never used to go *alone*," her mother said. "You had an escort."

"Well, I do tonight too," Joan said. "Frank Cotwell's going to meet me there and ride back with me."

"Frank Cotwell!" Her mother stared at her in amazement. "That's impossible! He's up in the mountains with your brother!"

"Not Dan, Mother. Frank—Dan's younger brother."

"You mean, you have a date with *another* of the

Cotwell boys?" Mrs. Drayfus' voice had taken on a shrill note. "It's not enough that Dan Cotwell lures your poor brother into the mountains, that he's up there now, lost, maybe even hurt! Now you're going to start dating another Cotwell! What kind of sister are you, Joan! Don't you care what's been done to your brother!"

"Dan wasn't responsible for Larry's going on that camping trip! I've told you that a hundred times! It was the other way around!" Joan fought to control her own voice. "Besides, I'm *not* dating Frank Cotwell. It's nothing like that at all. He's only a friend. He's two years younger than I am. All we're doing is going to the library!"

"Skip it tonight, Joanie." Her father spoke quietly. "It's not worth it if it upsets your mother."

"I can't skip it," Joan said. "I've promised."

"Then it *is* a date," her mother said. "If it weren't, you wouldn't be so stubborn about it!" Her voice was rising higher and higher. "I will not have you associating with that dreadful family! They ought to be arrested, every one of them! When Larry gets home, that's what we *will* have done—we'll have Dan arrested for kidnapping!"

"Kidnapping!" Joan repeated the word in stunned amazement. "You can't mean that!"

"I certainly do mean it!" Mrs. Drayfus turned to her husband. "Lawrence . . ."

"Now, Margaret, try to calm down, dear." Lawrence Drayfus met his daughter's eyes in helpless appeal. "Your mother is upset, Joan. If she asks you to stay home tonight, surely you can humor her. You can go to the library in the morning. Call the Cotwell boy and tell him your plans have changed. There shouldn't be any difficulty about that."

"I can't," Joan had said, her eyes moving from her mother's face to her father's, feeling the tight fingers of panic clutch at her heart. There must not be a scene—not with her mother as she was now—and yet, she could not give in! She had to be at the library at eight!

"Please," she said desperately, "I won't be late, I promise! I'll be back so soon you'll hardly know I'm gone! Mother—Daddy—I *have* to go!"

Her mother had burst into tears. Even now, hours later, she could hear the rasping sound of the sobs, could see the strained, exhausted look of her father's face, as he stood, torn between them, trying to mediate what was not even an argument but a scene of such emotional chaos that there was no reasonable end for it.

At last, it had been decided that Joan would go to the library "this once." Her father would drive her over and she would return by bus. She would be at home by nine-thirty.

"No later," her father had said. "Not even one minute later. Your mother isn't in a state to be made to worry."

"I know." She could not bear to see the pain in his eyes.

"She's not well, Joan. She'll be better soon. When the shock wears off, she'll be her old self again. Just be patient."

"Sure, Daddy. I'm sorry about tonight. I'll—this won't happen again." She reached over and touched the hand that was clenched so tightly around the steering wheel. "I'll be home at nine-thirty. Honestly."

It was a little after nine when the bus pulled to a stop at her corner.

Joan got to her feet, realizing suddenly that she had not thought to check out a book. Her parents would think it strange that she had returned without one. Still, it was too late now.

Perhaps they would not even notice. Perhaps her mother had the television on and would not even raise her face from its intent gaze upon the flickering screen. Everything was so strange now. Home was no longer home, her parents were no longer the people she had loved and depended upon for so many years. A shadow lay upon all of them.

Beside her, Frank had risen too.

"You don't have to get off here," Joan said. "You can ride a couple of blocks farther and get off at Maple."

"I'll walk you home."

"You don't have to do that. It's only a block."

"That's okay."

"No, really, Frank."

She put a hand on his shoulder and pressed him back into the seat. The one thing of which she was certain was that she could not allow him to see her to her door. Perhaps her mother would be buried in television, but there was the chance that she would not be. She might be there in the living room, her eyes fastened on the hands of the clock, watching nine-thirty grow nearer and nearer. If she saw Frank, appearing with Joan in the doorway, there might be another scene, even worse than the one at dinner. The tears, the hysterical accusations might come bursting forth with renewed violence.

"Thank you," she said now, quickly, "for meeting me there tonight. I wish I knew what happened."

"Maybe he'll call you again. If he does, you'll let me know?"

"Yes, of course."

The driver was regarding her impatiently.

"Thanks again, Frank," she said, and hurried down the steps to the street.

What could have gone wrong? She asked herself the question again as she began the walk along the sidewalk toward her house. None of the explanations she and Frank had offered each other were sound when you really examined them. It was all very well to say "things got twisted," but it was difficult to see how this could have happened.

She had not misunderstood either the time or the place. The more she thought about it, the more certain she was of this. Had the man changed his mind? Had he decided, upon second thought, that it would be a waste of time to meet with a teenage girl about such a large sum of money? Had he decided to go to her parents as he had first intended? Perhaps this very moment the telephone in the living room was ringing.

The thought of this lent speed to her feet. Her footsteps clicked faster and faster on the empty sidewalk until she was almost running. If the phone did ring, who would take it, her father or her mother? What would they say? How would they react?

"Miss Drayfus?"

The voice spoke quietly, but the words shot out to her through the darkness. Joan felt her heart give a leap of startled terror.

Where? How?

Then she saw the dark shape of the automobile parked beside the curb.

Her first impulse was to run. She could feel the muscles in her legs involuntarily contracting in preparation for flight.

"Miss Drayfus?" the voice said again. She recognized it now, or thought she did.

Slowly she turned to face the car.

"Mr. . . . Brown?"

"That's right."

The man in the automobile reached across from the driver's seat and opened the door next to the sidewalk. It was like an invitation, and Joan took an automatic step backward. Hurriedly she glanced about her. The street was empty, but lights blinked comfortingly from the front windows of houses both before and behind her. It was still early enough in the evening so that people had not settled themselves for sleeping. Windows were open to catch the movement of air; people would be reading and chatting, playing cards, watching television.

If she called for help, she would be heard, not by one person but by many. The whole neighborhood would hear her. As long as she stayed here on the sidewalk she was in no immediate danger.

"You weren't there," she said as steadily as she could. "I went to the library. I waited half an hour. You didn't come."

"You weren't alone," the man's voice said. "I had an appointment with *you*. I expected this to be a private discussion."

"You didn't tell me not to bring anybody," Joan said.

"I didn't think I had to. I couldn't imagine your being foolish enough to want your brother's—unorthodox— behavior spread all over the place." He sounded impatient. "Well, now you're rid of the boy friend, climb in. I'll show you the paper your brother signed."

"No." Joan backed away another step. "I'm not getting in the car. If you have something to show me, bring it out here. We'll walk down to the street light."

"What do you think I'm going to do, kidnap you?" The voice from the darkness of the car was thick with anger.

"I'm not getting into a strange car."

Turning on her heel, she began to walk toward the street light in the middle of the block. She kept her shoulders set, her eyes straight ahead. Behind her, she heard the slam of a car door. Had he gotten out, or was he preparing to drive away?

Her ears strained for the sound of footsteps on the sidewalk behind her.

She did not turn until she reached the pool of light. Then she did so, slowly, and he was there.

He was not a large man; in fact, he stood shorter than she. He had a thin, dark face behind metal-rimmed glasses. He was wearing a business suit, much like those her father wore when he went each morning to his job in the trust department of the bank.

"Look," Mr. Brown said quietly, "this is enough dramatics. I don't make a business of grabbing young girls. I'm here for one reason, to collect the money I have coming to me. Your brother disappeared owing me over two thousand dollars, and I intend to have it."

Joan pressed her hands tightly against her sides to keep them from trembling. She drew a deep breath.

"How do I know that Larry really owed you that much money?"

"That's simple to prove. I have his signature."

The man reached into his coat pocket and drew out a paper. He held it out to her, keeping at the same time a firm grip on the corner. The glow of the street light fell upon the page.

Leaning forward, Joan read the printed words:

Receipt for merchandise received.
Paid in full, $2,150.
Signed—Lawrence Drayfus, Jr.

It was Larry's signature. A glance was enough to tell her that. When she leaned closer, there was absolutely no doubt. She knew that writing, the way his "L" looped up in a high, easy wave and the odd, sharp points on the "r"s.

"What merchandise?" she asked. "What kind of business deal was this?"

"Miss Drayfus, I am in the jewelry business." He showed no hesitation at the question. "Your brother was working for me as a glorified delivery boy. Every other week he exported sample pieces of jewelry and designs from Mexico."

"Larry was doing that!" Joan exclaimed in astonishment. "He never mentioned it at home!"

"He had instructions not to," Mr. Brown told her. "This business is being conducted privately and as quietly as possible. Briefly, Miss Drayfus, the situation is this. Mexican-style jewelry is very much in demand in this country. Shops in the North and East will retail it at a very high markup. The problem is the duty that has to be paid when it is brought in quantity across the border.

"Here in New Mexico we have our own Pueblo Indians, many of whom are excellent silversmiths. Their labor is cheap, and the results very good. By having the Indians manufacture Mexican-style jewelry here in the States, we eliminate the duty, and out-of-state shops don't know the difference. This is *not* illegal, if that's what you're thinking. . . ." He caught the look on her face. "This is what is known as good business. The

Indians are paid, I am paid, and the shops make a good profit."

Joan regarded him with bewilderment.

"What did Larry have to do with all this?"

"It was Larry's job to drive down every other week to pick up new designs and sample pieces of jewelry from our agents in Juarez. He delivered them to me, and I, in turn, distributed them among the Indian craftsmen. It was a simple job, but it was good pay for a teen-ager."

"But, I don't understand," Joan said slowly. "Where did the two thousand dollars come from? Why would Larry have that kind of money in his possession?"

"That was because of my own bad judgment," Mr. Brown said wryly. "The boy had worked for us for a number of months, and he seemed honest and responsible. In early April, I offered him an opportunity for higher earnings by taking over the second leg of the job—delivering the samples to the Pueblo and bringing back their finished replicas. In the course of this, he was responsible for carrying the money to pay the Indians for their work, plus the raw materials, silver and turquoise."

"Two thousand dollars," Joan exclaimed.

"This is a business, Miss Drayfus. We deal in sums that far exceed that. In this case, however, the sum is sufficient for me to be very unhappy about the possibility of losing it. Your brother picked up the money from me at the end of the school week, with the understanding that he would make the trip to the Pueblo with it over the weekend. He never got there. Instead, according to the newspapers, he went camping in the Mogollons."

"He couldn't have made the trip that weekend,"

Joan said defensively. "My father wouldn't let him have the car. He didn't have any choice."

"Whatever the circumstances, Miss Drayfus, he managed to disappear with the money." The meaning in Mr. Brown's voice was clear.

Joan stared at him incredulously.

"Do you mean—are you trying to say—that Larry didn't go on a camping trip at all? That he *stole* that money and—and ran away with it?"

"From what I understand, a thorough search was made in the mountains. No trace of him was found."

"That doesn't prove a thing," Joan said angrily. "Those are wild mountains. They're part of the Wilderness Area! Other hikers have been lost up there and never found. What you're saying—that Larry is a thief —that he ran off—it's the most ridiculous thing I've ever heard! He would never do a thing like that, *never!"*

"In that case," Mr. Brown said quietly, "the money must be somewhere among his possessions."

"I suppose it must be. He certainly wouldn't take it on a camping trip with him."

"Then, Miss Drayfus, may I suggest that you make a search of his things and see if you can locate it?"

"Yes," Joan said, "I will. I'll go through everything. I can't imagine his leaving that large a sum just sitting around though. Perhaps he deposited it in the bank for safekeeping until he could make the trip to the Pueblo."

"That's a possibility," Mr. Brown agreed. "I'll give you a chance to check. If, however, you are unable to locate the money, I'm afraid I'll have no choice but to talk to your parents."

"My parents!" Those were the words that brought her back to reality. "Nine-thirty! I told them . . ." She raised her left wrist, trying to focus in the dim glow of the street light.

She caught her breath sharply.

"I'll look," she told the man with the glasses. "If it's there, I'll find it."

Without another word, she turned and began to run the distance of the half block that would take her home.

Six

Because both she and Larry, at twelve and ten years of age, had established savings accounts at the bank in whose trust department their father worked, it was here that Joan called first on the following Monday morning. She realized when she did so that she might very well be refused information concerning the balance of her brother's account.

She was unprepared, however, to find that the account had been closed out completely.

Why would he do that? She replaced the receiver in bewilderment. What had he done with the money the account contained? Perhaps, she thought suddenly, he had opened another account elsewhere. It was the sort of thing a teen-age boy might do in a moment of rebellion, establish his finances as far as possible from the association that represented his father. The possibility was at least worth investigation.

Twenty minutes later she had completed her calls. Not one of the banks listed in the Yellow Pages held an account, either checking or savings, for Lawrence Drayfus, Jr.

He probably closed it, Joan decided at last, because he spent all the money in it. This was in character, for to Larry, money had always been for spending. It was for this reason that Mr. Drayfus had insisted on the children's opening savings accounts in the first place. Birthday and Christmas checks from aunts and grandparents sifted through Larry's fingers in what seemed a matter of minutes. There was always "something special" upon which he needed to spend it—first candy and toys—then, as he grew older, shoes and clothing. Larry was a clotheshorse, and his wardrobe of slacks and sweaters and sports jackets was of excellent quality and infinite variety.

Although he enjoyed spending money, Larry had never held much interest in the prospect of earning it. While Joan systematically supplemented her allowance with earnings from baby-sitting and her summer job as camp counselor, Larry did not seem to worry about increasing his income. When he was fourteen, his father had insisted on his taking a job as a paper boy, mostly because Mr. Drayfus himself had held such a job in his teens.

"It'll be good for the boy," he had said firmly. "Get him outside in the fresh air—give him a feeling of accomplishment. There are a lot of opportunities connected with this sort of thing, all kinds of contests and things where newsboys win trips to Europe."

The job had not worked out, Larry had stuck with it for less than a month, complaining bitterly the entire time. In the end it had turned out to be Mrs. Drayfus who did the major part of the paper delivery, driving Larry along his route because the weather was "wet" or "cold" or Larry wasn't "feeling well," and sometimes taking over the morning delivery entirely because Larry's alarm clock "did not go off" in time for him to get the job completed before school.

Larry's job with Mr. Brown was the first Joan had ever known of his finding work for himself.

Because of these things, it was not, she told herself, surprising that her brother should close out his savings account. He had probably spent what was in it and had no inclination to continue with a savings program. The money from Mr. Brown must, therefore, if it existed at all, be some place among his possessions in his room.

To search Larry's room was a simple enough decision. It was less simple, Joan discovered, to force herself to turn the doorknob and walk inside. Larry's room had always been his own and no one else's. He had had a special sense of privacy about his things, which the rest of the family, from long experience, respected. He had kept his door closed at all times, and, as far as Joan knew, even their mother had ventured inside only to bring clean laundry and make up his bed for him.

"Well, Larry's gone now," Joan told herself firmly, "and there's no helping this. It's something I have to do."

Bracing herself, she turned the knob and opened the door, stepped through, and drew it closed behind her.

Larry's room, as it lay before her, was as neat and well kept as the boy himself had been. It had not been touched in any way since his departure for the fatal camping trip, and there was a waiting, expectant feeling about it, as though Larry might be returning to it at any moment. The bed was neatly made; the alarm clock on the bedside table was set for seven-thirty, the usual rising time for a school morning. The bureau top was immaculate, with comb and brush arranged there at a precise angle, and a framed photograph, an enlargement of Larry's junior class picture, set to the left of the mirror. It was the only picture in the room.

Looking around her at the sterile neatness, Joan

found herself contrasting it with the cluttered warmth of her own room down the hall. School posters, colored throw pillows, souvenirs and pennants seemed to blossom from every corner. Pictures looked out at one from all angles—a bulletin board, the desk, the bureau top—formal photographs of her parents and of Larry, snapshots of school friends, Scouts she had counseled the previous summer, pets from years back, barking and mewing and quacking in various poses in the back yard.

And, of course, on the bedside table stood a picture of Dan. It was the one that had been taken for the yearbook, and it showed him looking very solemn, his chin set, his eyes straight ahead. It was not her favorite picture of him, but it was the most recent, and he had given it to her only a week before he left to go camping.

"A rogues' gallery," her father referred to the array teasingly. "How do you ever get to sleep with all those faces staring out at you?"

"I manage." Joan had laughed. "I like mobs."

But Larry had had only one picture to gaze at him at night—his own.

Larry, Larry, I wish we had been closer! I wish I could feel I'd really known you!

Joan picked up the photograph, turning it in her hands so that the eyes smiled into her own. Unlike Dan's, which was solemn and posed, Larry's yearbook picture was a good one. It had caught the elusive, elfin quality of the quicksilver grin, the suggestion of dimples, still faint in the childlike curve of the recently thinned cheeks. The face was beautiful, but the boy behind the face—who had he been, really? What had he thought and felt? What was he laughing about?

We'll never know. It's too late. I should have tried harder, talked to him more, asked his opinions of things.

Other sisters manage to be close to their brothers. Anne Tonjes' brother is only thirteen, but they talk about everything together. If only I'd made more effort . . .

Well, it's too late now.

Regretfully, she set the picture back into place and drew open the top drawer of the bureau.

The insides of Larry's drawers echoed the compulsive neatness of the rest of his room, and a complete exploration took only a matter of minutes. Socks, pajamas, and underwear lay in separate piles, needing only to be lifted and dropped back into place. In the second drawer, shirts were arranged in careful order; in the third were piles of precisely folded sweaters.

One by one, Joan lifted and checked each item, feeling through the soft cotton of T-shirts, running her fingers inquiringly into the folds of socks. Everything was exactly as it appeared on the surface. There were no hidden papers of any kind, no bankbooks, and certainly no money.

The next step was the closet. Again, when she opened the door, Larry's neatness stared back at her. His winter suits hung, clean and pressed, on their hangers. Sports shirts followed, then white shirts, then slacks, folded with care so that their creases fell in exact alignment. Nothing was mussed or crowded. In the bag on the door, Larry's shoes were arranged in correct compartments.

Carefully, Joan thumbed her way through the clothing, feeling in the pockets of slacks and shirts and in the compartments of the shoe bag. There was nothing.

From the closet she went to the bed, folded back the bedclothes, and searched under the mattress.

By this time the whole procedure was beginning to seem ridiculous. Where next, she asked herself contemptuously. Under the rug? Inside the pillow case? Behind the books in the bookcase?

Absurd, completely absurd—and yet . . .

"Receipt for merchandise received. Paid in full, $2,150. Signed—Lawrence Drayfus, Jr."

Absurd or not, the signature on the receipt had been Larry's. Somewhere two thousand one hundred and fifty dollars existed.

Drawing a long breath, Joan squared her shoulders and continued the search. Yes, she would look under the rug, in the pillow case, anywhere, everywhere. If the money was in this room, she would find it. She had to.

It was almost a full hour later when she permitted herself to admit defeat. With a sigh, she sank to a sitting position on the foot of Larry's bed. She had covered every corner of the room, not once but several times. She could swear that there was not an inch—under things, within things, on closet shelves, in drawers—that she had not searched thoroughly. There was nothing in the room that should not have been there. There was nothing suspicious in any way. And there was definitely no two thousand dollars.

Where else would he have put it, if not in his room?

She turned her eyes, once more, to the photograph on the dresser, as though in that smiling face she might find an answer.

"Where?" she asked silently. "Where is it, Larry? You must have put it some place for safekeeping."

The eyes smiled back at her, inscrutable behind their veil of laughter.

If she herself had not known Larry, was there anyone who had? The very lack of pictures in the sterile room seemed to indicate that there had not been. She had always taken for granted, without much thought, the fact that Larry, like herself, had numerous friends scattered about through his classes at school. It was strange how few of his classmates had phoned or come by with concern and condolences when he was reported missing. The telephone had rung constantly, yes. Her mother's words sprang again to her mind: "Larry must have a lot of friends. There have been so many calls." But now, when she thought back upon it, she realized with surprise that almost all the calls had been from her own friends or friends of her parents.

Had Larry had any close friends? With whom had he spent his time when he was not at home? Try though she would, Joan could not come up with a single name. Her parents' friends, she knew, had doted upon him; he had always known, better than she, exactly what to do to charm older people. But as far as his own contemporaries were concerned, he had never seemed to consider them important enough to be worth the effort. As far as she knew, that disastrous party at the Brownings', at which the police had intervened, was the first social event he had taken the trouble to attend all year.

It was a strange, almost frightening realization, coming now, as it did, with Larry gone. How alone he had been, always! To have grown up with him, to have lived in the same house with him, and not to have realized—

"Joan!" Her mother's voice broke through her consciousness. "Joan, where are you?"

Hurriedly, Joan got up from the bed and crossed the room. She was just stepping through the door when her mother appeared at the far end of the hallway. She stood there, frozen, as though unable to believe her eyes.

"What . . . ?" She brought out the question in a

croaking voice. "What have you been doing in your brother's room?"

"Nothing. Just—just looking over his things." Joan was amazed at her own quick flush of guilt. "It's something that will have to be done, Mother. We can't just leave everything there indefinitely."

"You know Larry doesn't allow people to go into his room," Mrs. Drayfus said accusingly. "You know how he loves his privacy."

"Larry's gone," Joan said gently.

"He'll be back soon. He'll be furious if he finds that you've been rummaging through his things, Joan. I'm surprised at you."

She really believes it—that he will be coming home again! Joan stared at the woman who was her mother, pity swelling in her heart.

You have me! she ached to cry to her. Mother—look at me—please! Remember, you have me still!

But she knew that if she spoke the words aloud, her mother would not hear them. Mrs. Drayfus was not with her now. She was staring past her through the open doorway into the empty room beyond. Her eyes held that lost, glazed look as they did so often lately, as though she had withdrawn from them all into a world where Larry's shadow was stronger, brighter than the reality of either her daughter or husband.

For a moment, last Saturday night, Joan had thought that she might have broken through to her. She had come downstairs in the long, white gown with the odd, square cap on her head, to find her parents sitting in the living room.

Giving them both a bright smile, she had asked, "How do I look?"

"Like a sweet Girl Graduate," her father had said

with an answering smile. It was a tired smile, but there was warmth in his eyes. "I'm proud of you, honey. Look, Margaret—look at Joan in her cap and gown! Remember when she was in diapers? Lord—how many millions of years ago that seems! And now, she's graduating!"

"Joan—graduating?" Mrs. Drayfus had repeated the words, as though trying to grasp their meaning. "When?"

"Tonight, Mother!" Joan had gone over to her, speaking gently, as one might to a bewildered child. "This is graduation night. Don't you want to come and see me get my diploma?"

"Of course she does!" Mr. Drayfus had turned to his wife hopefully. "This is the biggest night in Joanie's life. We wouldn't miss it for anything, would we, Margaret?"

"I'm not dressed," Mrs. Drayfus had said slowly, her eyes dropping to her housecoat. It was the first time in weeks that she had seemed to take notice of what she was wearing.

Joan's heart lifted.

"That's all right. There's plenty of time. You'll have time to change."

"All right," Mrs. Drayfus said. "If Larry gets home in time."

She spoke so naturally, so matter-of-factly, that Joan could not believe she had understood the words.

She repeated them slowly.

"If Larry . . ."

"I can't go without Larry," her mother said stubbornly. "What if he should call while we are all gone? Or if he should come home and find nobody here?"

"But, Mother!" She could not answer. She turned her

face away, and her father got up wearily and came over and put an arm around her shoulders.

"I'm sorry, honey," he said softly. "I hoped, for a minute there . . ."

"I know. So did I."

"I'll be there." He tightened his arm around her. "I may be a little late, but I'll be there. I'll call around, see if I can get somebody to come over and stay here while I'm gone. I don't like leaving her alone in the evening, but I'm sure I can work things out somehow."

"That's all right. I understand." Joan had kept the disappointment from showing in her voice. "You stay right here and look after Mother. I'll know you're there in spirit. That's what matters."

"Well, if you're sure you won't mind." He sounded relieved. "Do you have a way to get to the auditorium?"

"Oh yes. The graduates have to get there early. Anne and her folks are coming by for me. They'll bring me home afterward." She had even managed to smile at him. "Don't expect a whole bunch of honors like Anne's going to get, but I will have the precious piece of parchment that says I made it through twelve glorious years!"

So she had gone with the Tonjeses to receive her diploma. It had been good to be with the Tonjes family, who were so happy and excited about Anne's triumphs as valedictorian and winner of one of the top scholarships. In the fall she was to start classes at U.C.L.A.

"What are your plans, dear?" Mrs. Tonjes asked kindly, and Joan shook her head.

"I don't know. The university, I suppose." The whole idea of college seemed to belong to another world, a normal, happy, promise-filled world that had existed a long time ago.

There were parties scheduled for the hours after the

graduation ceremony. Anne, who had taken it for granted that Joan would attend them, was concerned at her refusal.

"You don't need a date, if that's what's worrying you. A lot of people won't have them. The whole class will be going, just as a final farewell get-together. Come on, Joanie. My date will drive you home afterward."

"Thanks, but I can't," Joan said. "Really."

Anne regarded her with sympathy. "Dan was a wonderful guy. I know how it was with the two of you. But you can't just lock yourself away from everything, hon. He wouldn't have wanted you to miss out on graduation night. He'd have wanted you to go with us, you know that."

"I do know that," Joan said. "That's not the reason. It's Mother. You've seen her, Anne. She's just . . . not like herself. I don't like to be away from home for very long at a time."

"I thought she was getting better," Anne said. "At least, that's what your father told me the last time I called."

"I know. He says that to everyone. I think he's trying to convince himself. He thinks it's just a matter of adjustment, that once the initial shock is over she'll be her old self again."

"But you don't think so?" Anne asked worriedly.

"I don't know. I hope so. Sometimes she *does* seem better." She had spoken the words in a kind of desperation, but now, standing in the hallway, gazing at the woman before her, she knew that they were just that—words. No matter what she and her father told each other in love and hope, Mrs. Drayfus was *not* improving. Many people suffered from shock following a tragedy, but the numbness did not last—it wore off, gradually, bit by bit as they began to accept the pain of reality. With her mother, this acceptance had not come. She was, rather, slipping further and further away with each passing day into some far place where Larry lived still, laughing and beautiful, and it was her husband and daughter who were shadows.

"Mother . . ."

Joan did not know what she would have said if, at that moment, the doorbell had not rung.

For a moment it seemed that Mrs. Drayfus had not heard it. Then, abruptly, she cocked her head to one side.

"The bell," she said. "He must have forgotten his key."

"Who?" Joan asked, uncomprehending.

"Larry, of course. He must have forgotten it."

"It's the middle of the day, Mother," Joan said gently, her heart flooded with pity. "The door isn't locked in the daytime. It's somebody calling—a salesman, perhaps. I'll get it."

She turned and hurried down the stairs, hopeful that her mother was not following her.

This can't go on, she thought miserably. She can't continue this way. There must be something we can do. Perhaps, if we talk to a doctor . . .

When she was at the foot of the stairs the doorbell rang again. Joan opened the door quickly and stopped in surprise.

Frank Cotwell was standing on the doorstep.

"Why, Frank—hello."

There in the bright sunlight, his hair a cinnamon bristle, the freckles standing out in dark spots against his nose, he looked for an instant so much like Dan that her heart gave a painful leap and then settled again, heavily, in her chest. It was not Dan, steady and sure of himself, his blue eyes twinkling. It was only Frank, his face flushed with a combination of heat and embarrassment, his eyes dropping from hers as he fumbled for words.

"It's so hot," he said awkwardly, "I thought . . . well, the guys were telling me the other day, the public pool is open. I thought I'd go over and take a swim and . . . well, I was thinking, if you were hot too, you might want to go."

"Thanks, Frank. That's nice of you, but I—"

She had the answer half spoken when suddenly from the hall behind her she heard a startled gasp.

"Dan! Dan Cotwell! It's Dan!"

"Mother, no! It isn't Dan, it's his brother!"

Joan turned, but her mother was already rushing forward, crowding into the doorway beside her.

"Where's Larry? Where's my son? Dan, what have you done with my boy?"

"Larry?" Frank stared at her in bewilderment. "Larry's gone, Mrs. Drayfus, you know that. Larry and Dan, both. The police said—"

"Where is he? Don't pretend to me. How could you have come back without Larry? You've left him up there in the mountains—sick—maybe hurt. Where is he? Tell me this minute!"

Mrs. Drayfus' voice rose, high and painful, on a note Joan had not heard before. If she had not held out an arm to restrain her, her mother would have thrown herself on top of the confused boy.

"Mother, no! He isn't—really"—Joan threw Frank a pleading glance—"tell her . . ."

But he misinterpreted.

"Larry's dead, Mrs. Drayfus. After all this time, there

isn't any hope for them. The police say so—the rangers —everybody. He and Dan are dead."

He faltered and fell into silence, his eyes widening at the sight of the woman's face.

"Joan," he whispered, "didn't she *know?*"

A long scream broke the air, and Joan's arms went tight around her mother, catching her as she fell.

"Help me," she said, "Frank, help me. We've got to get her into her room and call my father—and a doctor!"

Seven

As spring slid into summer, so did June slip past and become the first hot days of July.

Mrs. Drayfus' roses bloomed and drooped and bloomed again and hung at last, heavy and brown on their tired stems, as though asking to be allowed to fall to the ground in peace.

The Cotwells' small house gathered the morning heat and held it close within itself while the sun moved in a high arch above its roof. Daylight clung to the sky for long hours after dinner was over, and the cool of the evening settled, finally, like a happy surprise, with the first stars shining steady and pale in the slowly darkening sky.

"What will we do on the Fourth?" Eddie asked.

Frank, who was sprawled on the chaise longue in the back yard, did not bother to answer. He had come outside to be alone, to escape from the bustle of family and the need to make conversation. Now, here was Eddie, crouched in the grass at his feet, asking his usual string of inane questions.

"Do you want to have a cookout like we did last year?"

"No," Frank said shortly, "I don't want to have a cookout."

"We could get some fireworks and shoot them off in the canyon. Chris Bryant has some his uncle brought back from their vacation trip."

"It's against the law," Frank said, "to shoot fireworks in New Mexico."

"I know, but we did it last year anyway. Gee, last year you thought it was great! Nobody's going to catch us in the canyon. We could take some hot dogs and—"

"Scram, will you, Eddie? Just scram." The words came out so vehemently that his own voice frightened him. "Just go somewhere, won't you?"

"Where?" Eddie lifted a hurt face.

"Anywhere. I don't care. Go take a walk, go visit somebody, go read a book or watch television. Heck, go anywhere, but just let me be! Can't a guy ever be alone around here?"

"Okay. Gee whiz. I just thought, with the Fourth so close and everything . . ."

Eddie got to his feet. There was something about the droop of his shoulders, the vulnerability of long arms and legs on the skinny boy's body that caught for an instant at Frank's heart.

He started to speak, to call him back, and then Eddie said, "Gee whiz, you're no fun at all any more. You act so snarly all the time. I wouldn't want to cook out with you, even if you wanted to."

"Great," Frank snapped. "Because I *don't* want to. So—scram."

"You didn't have to be so hard on him, Frankie."

His mother's voice spoke from the back doorway. She opened the screen door and came outside, crossing over to him.

"He's just lonesome."

"Yeah. Yeah, I know. He just . . . gets to me."

Frank started to get up, and his mother put out a restraining hand.

"Don't. Stay put. Do you mind if I sit with you for a few minutes? Dad had to go out on a service call tonight, and the house seems so empty."

"Sure, Mom. Sit down." Frank felt ashamed of himself. "Don't you want this chair where you can put your feet up?"

"Oh no. This one's fine. If I got into that one I might never be able to hoist myself out again."

His mother sank down with a sigh into the green and white plastic chair and leaned back to look up at the stars.

"It's a nice night. So clear and cool. You wouldn't guess it had been so hot during the day."

"We ought to get an air conditioner," Frank said.

"It would be nice, wouldn't it? Well, maybe next year. Till then, it helps just knowing the evenings are coming."

"You do too much," Frank said. "You run around too much in the heat. All that baking and stuff—you don't have to do that, Mom. That pie tonight and everything."

"You hardly touched it," Mrs. Cotwell said. "Eddie was the only one who ate it, and even he doesn't eat like he ought to for a growing boy. Oh, don't worry about me, Frankie. I like to keep busy. Baking keeps my mind off things. It keeps me from doing my own worrying."

There was a long pause.

Then Frank said, "About Dan? Mom, surely you *know*—"

"I know. Sure, I know. I don't worry about Danny any longer." His mother's voice was quiet. "It's my other boys I worry about now. About you, Frankie. You're not yourself any longer. You're so quiet all the time. You're pulling away from us. What is it, son? Is it Mrs. Drayfus—her getting sick while you were there and everything?"

"I guess so." Frank tried to keep his voice even. "When I think what I did! *I* did it, Mom—I was the one! It was seeing me there in the doorway. You should have seen her face, like I was a ghost. And then she screamed."

"She was a sick woman, dear. She had to be, in the first place, or she wouldn't have reacted that way. You didn't do it. You were just there."

"But, I *did* do it. I was the one who told her that Larry was dead. I didn't have to do that. If I hadn't said anything, if I'd just given her a few minutes to see that I really wasn't Dan, then Joan could have talked to her."

"But Larry *is* dead," his mother said gently. "Like Dan. It's been two and a half months now. If they were alive, we would have had some word about them by now. It's a heartbreaking thing, but we have to accept it.

"Mrs. Drayfus couldn't have gone on hiding from the fact indefinitely. There had to be a point where she realized it, and whenever that happened, it would have been just as bad. Maybe, if she had gone on the way she was, it would have been worse."

"She fainted," Frank said. "At least, that's what I think happened. She went all limp, and Joan grabbed her and held her up and yelled at me to help her. We carried her into her room and laid her on the bed. She was so light. I didn't know she was such a little woman. Joan could have carried her by herself, I think."

He paused, the memory flooding through him.

"Joan went to the telephone to call the doctor, and while she was calling, Mrs. Drayfus opened her eyes and looked up at me. She screamed. I never heard a woman scream before. She just lay there, looking at me and screaming and screaming."

He shuddered, sudden sickness churning in his stomach.

"Gosh, it was awful!"

"I can imagine," Mrs. Cotwell said softly. "It must have been."

"Joan tried to quiet her. She had me go into the living room, where Mrs. Drayfus wouldn't see me. She told me to call her father. I phoned him at his office, and he came—he must have driven like a demon all the way, because he got home by the time the doctor arrived. The doctor gave Mrs. Drayfus a shot of some kind, and she stopped screaming, but she was crying. A funny kind of crying, like she never would stop. The doctor said she had to go to the hospital.

"They put her in the car. They had a blanket around her like it was cold outside. Like it wasn't the middle of the summer."

"Poor thing," his mother said softly. "Poor, poor woman."

"All I wanted to do," Frank said brokenly, "was to take Joan swimming. I was sorry for her and—and after all, she was Dan's girl friend and—it was so hot . . ."

"I know. I know, son. You couldn't possibly have known what would happen." His mother sighed. "Poor woman. I wish there was something we could do to help."

"Why did it hit her like that, Mom?" Frank asked. "I know she had a shock, hearing about Larry, but you did too. Dan's gone too, and he was *your* son, and you cried and all, sure, but you didn't go all apart like that. You're here baking pies and stuff. You're able to sit here in the yard and talk about it."

"Nobody can tell the 'why' of these things," his mother said. "I guess I'm luckier than Mrs. Drayfus. I'm made differently. Some of us are built like china cups and some like plastic mugs."

Frank digested the comparison.

"I'm glad you're a mug," he said gratefully. "What would we do if *you* smashed up?"

"Just what Joan and her father are doing, I suppose. Make the best of it and try to get me mended. How are they doing, Frank? Have you been over there since Mrs. Drayfus . . . went away?"

"No. I . . . I couldn't. I know I should have but . . ." Frank did not even attempt to make excuses. "I phoned Joan a couple of days later. She said they'd taken her mother to a place—it's not exactly a hospital—it's more like a private nursing home where people go when they have breakdowns. Her friend Anne was over there with her when I called, and she sounded like she didn't want to go into it. I couldn't blame her. I'd think she'd never want to talk to me again."

"You couldn't have known." His mother's voice was very gentle. "You're a good boy, Frank—the best. You wouldn't hurt anyone if you could help it."

"It's Dan who was the best," Frank said ruefully, "Dan wouldn't have done something so darned clumsy.

Dan always knew just what to say to people. Everything he did was always so—so—*right*."

"Dan was one of those lucky people," Mrs. Cotwell said. "He was born with a way about him, a security, a kind of knowing. He was a good boy too, but no better than you, son. Life is a little harder for you, that's all. You have to learn the things he was born knowing. But you'll have a chance to learn them. And Eddie too.

"You must be patient with Eddie. Dan used to pay him so much attention, and now, with him gone, he needs you more than he does the rest of us. We all need each other."

"Sure we do. I'm sorry, Mom. I guess I've been thinking too much about myself and not enough about Eddie and the rest of you."

Frank was glad of the gradually descending darkness, which hid his face. He raised a hand and brushed it across his eyes.

"The Fourth—well, why don't I take the kid on a cookout like he wants? I can do that. It might even be fun once we got there."

"Maybe we could all go," his mother suggested. "We could make a family thing out of it like we used to do. Some of your friends—Roger, maybe, and Scott Kimball—they might like to go with us."

"Sure. Swell. I'll ask them."

He paused and glanced up at the rustle of footsteps approaching around the side of the house.

"Eddie?"

"It's Joan."

The voice spoke out of the shadows an instant before the girl herself appeared, silhouetted against the light from the kitchen windows.

"I rang the front doorbell, but no one answered, and I thought maybe you were sitting out back here. I hope you don't mind."

"We're glad to see you, Joan," Mrs. Cotwell said warmly. "Sit down and join us. Frank and I were just cooling off a little. How is your mother?"

"The doctors say we shouldn't look for any real changes too quickly." Joan seated herself on the glider across from Frank. "They say it takes time for emotions to heal up, just like it does for the body itself. You wouldn't expect somebody to come out of a car accident, all perfect again, overnight. But she's getting treatment, and she's going to get better. The doctors seem sure of it. I—I hope they're right."

"You're a brave girl, Joan," Mrs. Cotwell said approvingly.

Hearing her, Frank thought again of her reference to the china cup and the plastic mug. The mug was not as beautiful on first sight, but when stresses came, it stood strong. Could this have been the quality that Dan saw when he turned away from a dozen prettier girls to settle his heart upon Joan Drayfus?

Now he looked at her with new respect as she said, "Not so brave really. There are times—"

She let the sentence break.

"I know," Mrs. Cotwell said softly. "There are those times for us all."

Giving herself a little shake, she got to her feet.

"I think I'll go in and fix some iced tea. Would you young people like some?"

"Thank you," Joan said. "That sounds wonderful."

"Frank?"

"Yes, thanks, Mom. Do you want me to help you?"

He had already swung his feet over the side of the

chaise when his mother said, "Of course not. You sit right there and talk to Joan. Since when does it take two people to make iced tea?"

"I just thought . . ."

Now it was he who did not complete a sentence. The truth was, and his mother knew it as well as he did, that he dreaded the thought of being left alone with Joan Drayfus. To face her again, after their last tragic encounter, was difficult enough, even with his mother present.

Now, leaning back in the chair, listening to the brisk sound of her retreating footsteps as she mounted the kitchen steps, he felt utterly deserted.

The screen door opened and banged closed, and then there was silence. A long silence, a stillness so heavy that the drone of night insects sounded loud in the honeysuckle along the back fence. Music from a radio floated over from one of the houses behind them.

"Joan—"

"Frank—"

They spoke at the same time, stopped, laughed.

"What were you going to say?" Joan asked him.

"Nothing that you don't already know, I guess. Just that, I'm sorry. About your mother—my part of it. I was such a dope."

"You haven't been blaming yourself, have you?" Joan asked in surprise. "Why, you weren't responsible. It would have happened anyway, her breaking down like that. The doctor, when he heard about everything that led up to it, was surprised that it hadn't happened sooner."

"I'm glad." Frank let out his breath in relief, and then, horrified at his own words, amended them hastily.

"What I mean is, I'm glad it wasn't just because of me."

"The person I'm worried about now," Joan said, "is my father. All this is a terrific strain on him. But he seems to be holding up wonderfully. Just knowing that Mother is getting help seems to have lifted a weight off his shoulders."

She paused and then said, "I talked to Mr. Brown last night."

"You what?" Frank was startled. "You mean the guy who phoned you and then never showed up? Did he call you again?"

"You're behind on things," Joan said. "He *did* show up. I haven't had a chance to tell you about it, but he followed me, that night, after we left the library. When I got off the bus he was there, waiting in his car."

"My gosh!" Frank exclaimed in horror. "I should have walked home with you! You shouldn't have been by yourself!"

"If I hadn't been, he wouldn't have talked to me," Joan said. "Don't sound so worried. He didn't try to do a thing to me. All he did was talk. He showed me the receipt with Larry's signature. It *was* his signature, Frank. I don't have any doubt of that. He was really involved in business with this man, and he had a large amount of money in his possession at the time he went camping with Dan."

"Did he tell you what this business was?" Frank asked her.

Joan nodded. Briefly she outlined the conversation with Mr. Brown.

"He was supposed to go out to the Pueblo that weekend," she concluded, "but, of course, he couldn't. Dad had clamped down on him because of the party at the

Brownings', and he wasn't allowed to take the car. That's why he was so keen on the camping trip. He knew it was the only way he'd get out of the house that weekend. Larry couldn't stand being tied down and restricted."

"He couldn't have taken the money with him," Frank said. "Nobody would haul cash like that along in a knapsack!"

"It doesn't seem reasonable," Joan agreed. "Still, I'm beginning to wonder if he might not have done exactly that. I've called the banks—the one where he used to have a savings account and all of the others in town as well—and he hasn't deposited the money anywhere. I've been through his room from one end to the other. There's no money there, Frank. That two thousand dollars has vanished completely."

"And last night Mr. Brown called back to find out about it?"

"Yes," Joan said. "He was pretty angry. I gather he'd called a number of times before that and got no answer. Daddy and I have been out a lot lately. He thought we might have moved or left town."

"What did he say," Frank asked, "when you told him you couldn't find the money?"

"He thinks . . ." Joan paused. "It's so ridiculous I hate to even tell you. He thinks that Larry didn't go on a camping trip at all. He thinks he took the money and ran away."

"That's crazy," Frank exclaimed. "Ran away? And Dan along with him, I suppose? Letting us all believe they're up on the mountain, lost? Letting their folks go crazy worrying and grieving—shoving your mother into a sanitarium! All for two thousand dollars? Why, Dan wouldn't do such a thing for a million times that much!"

"Of course he wouldn't," Joan agreed heartily, "and Larry wouldn't either. Only some kind of monster would do that. The point is, he mustn't be allowed to suggest such a thing to my parents. I don't know how much further Daddy can be pushed, and as for Mother —she's only now beginning to learn to adjust herself to the idea of Larry's death. What would it do to her if, somehow, she learned about this?"

"Is that what he threatened?" Frank asked angrily. "To tell your parents?"

"It was at first. I tried to explain to him, to plead with him. I told him I would pay back the money myself as quickly as I could, that I was going to start looking for a job immediately. I don't have training in anything special. I've always planned eventually on being a teacher. Of course, I don't have the schooling for that yet, but I'm sure I could find something I could do.

"That's when he changed." A puzzled note crept into her voice. "He stopped sounding angry and seemed to get more understanding. It was as though he were thinking something over. And then he offered me a job."

"A job? Working for *him*?" Frank said in surprise. "Doing what, for Pete's sake?"

"Actually, what he offered me was the same job Larry had, picking up jewelry samples and designs from his associates in Mexico. It's only once every other week."

"You're thinking of taking this?"

"I don't know how I can afford not to," Joan told him. "As I say, I have no training in anything. The best I could hope to find around Las Cruces would be work in a dime store or soda fountain or something. It would take my entire day and maybe even into the evening. The delivery job for Mr. Brown would take only one day every two weeks, a two-hour drive down and two hours back again. That way, I'd be free to go to see Mother at the nursing home, and when she's well enough to come home, I'll be there to take care of her."

"And what is he offering to pay for this cushy job?" Frank asked skeptically.

"He's going to allow me to work off Larry's debt at fifty dollars a trip."

"Fifty dollars a trip, just to flit down to Mexico!" Frank could not restrain his astonishment. "Something doesn't ring right here! This jewelry you're bringing back, what does it consist of? This could be some kind of smuggling operation."

"No," Joan said, "it can't be, Frank. The jewelry is just sample pieces, of no great value in themselves. I'm to take them through customs and declare them. The really important thing is the designs that go with them, the ones that will be used by the Indian silversmiths.

"I know it sounds funny, but I honestly believe that offering me this opportunity is Mr. Brown's way of being kind. As crazy and mixed up as this whole situation is, people don't really like to hurt people."

"I don't like anything about it," Frank said shortly. "The whole business, if you can call it that, sounds slippery. Otherwise, why would this guy be trying to keep it all so secret? Calling himself Mr. John Brown, arranging mysterious meetings. Honest people don't act that way."

"Honest people don't disappear with other people's

money either," Joan said quietly, "but Larry seems to have done so. And Larry was honest, Frank. He was my brother, and I can't believe anything else of him. There's a lot of wheeling and dealing behind any business. Everybody tries to figure out ways of beating the competition. Even in the trust department where my father works, the whole idea is to avoid taxes and beat other people to investments. I'm sure that Daddy knows a lot of secrets and uses them to help his clients, but that doesn't make him dishonest."

"I'm glad my own dad is a television repairman. It's all out and open. He either fixes sets or he doesn't." Frank drew a long breath. "Well, if you're set on it, I guess that's that. When do we make our first trek to Mexico?"

"*We?*" Joan said in surprise. "Why, you don't have to go, Frank. I'm a good driver, and Daddy will let me use the car anytime I ask him. This is my problem, not yours."

"You don't think I'd let you go down alone, do you?" Frank asked gruffly. "That's just empty desert, between here and Mexico. Besides, those border towns are pretty rough places. Women shouldn't wander around in them by themselves."

"I'd be all right. I'm sure I would." Joan paused, and then said more softly, "Why, Frank?"

"Why, what?"

"Why are you being so nice to me? I thought— I mean, back when Dan was alive—I sometimes thought you didn't like me very much."

"That's crazy," Frank said, feeling the hot blood rush to his face. He blessed the cool blanket of concealing darkness. "You were Dan's girl friend, weren't you? Dan would want me to—to kind of look after you."

"Thank you," Joan said softly. She reached across impulsively and laid her hand on his where it rested on the arm of the chaise longue.

"That's okay," Frank said.

They sat for a while in comfortable silence, and it was not until his mother came out with the iced tea that he made the effort to draw his hand away.

Eight

"Excuse me." The girl's voice spoke from close beside him. "Could you tell me the time?"

Dave raised his head from the beach towel, blinking against the blinding glare of the white sand. The girl was standing over him, silhouetted against the high, rich curve of sky.

He dropped his eyes to his watch.

"Two-thirty. At least, close to it. This thing doesn't keep the most perfect time."

"Thanks. That gives me a few more minutes before I have to start thinking about getting ready for work." Her voice was easy and pleasantly low pitched. "I'm sorry if I disturbed you. You seemed to be the only person on the whole beach who was wearing a wrist watch."

"You didn't disturb me. I'd better get a shirt on or I'm going to turn into a cooked lobster."

Dave sat up and reached for the T-shirt that lay beside the towel. All about him the sand shimmered in the afternoon heat, but the sea breeze was cool against his face.

"I'm from New York," he said. "I'm not used to this California sunshine."

"You don't sound like New York," the girl commented.

"I don't?" The remark caught him by surprise. He raised his eyes again, taking in the tall slimness of her figure, the straight brown legs beneath the red knit swimming suit. "What *do* I sound like? Where would you think I was from?"

"I don't know. I haven't heard you talk enough."

"Sit down for a few minutes. Maybe you can make a guess."

He offered the suggestion lightly, but even as he did so he knew that he was not casual about wanting the girl to stay. There was something about her, about the low voice, the tall, well-proportioned figure, that brought with it a flash of recognition.

"Haven't I met you before some place?" he asked, and then flushed at the practiced sound of the question.

"I don't think so." She sounded amused, but she did drop down to a kneeling position on the sand beside him. "Did you think that approach up all by yourself?"

"No, I must have read it somewhere." He smiled at her. "Really, I mean it. I'm sure I've seen you. Maybe at the beach last weekend?"

"Possibly. I'm here a lot during the summer. My family has a house just a couple of blocks from the beach."

The girl smiled back at him. There was a friendly naturalness about her that compensated for her lack of conventional prettiness. Her straight brown hair was pushed back from her face and caught by a white band; her mouth was wide, her gray eyes set far apart, her brows and lashes bleached by the sun until they were almost invisible against the tan of her face.

"Are you here in California on vacation?"

"Well, not exactly." Before the girl's wide gaze, Dave found himself loath to admit to having been ill enough to have made the move from one coast to another. "We live here now. We have a room at the Royal Palm Apartments."

"We?" Her eyes flicked quickly to his left hand, as though seeking the gold of a wedding band.

"My younger brother and I," Dave said quickly. He gestured out toward the rolling blue waves, their crests dotted with brown-skinned surfers. "Lance seems to have found his place in life. We've only been here a couple of months, and he's already king of the beach boys. I hardly see him from morning till night. One of those specks out there now on top of a wave is him."

"Why aren't you out there with him?" the girl asked curiously. "You look as though you'd be good at sports."

"I'm working my way up to it gradually."

He did not add that his slowly returning strength had made the thought of taking on a new sport more of a chore than a pleasure. It was only in the past few days that he had begun to look upon the antics of the surfers with any real interest.

Now, before the girl's question, he said, "It does look like it would be fun. Maybe I will take a try at it one one of these days."

"I can teach you, if you like. I was born here, and I've been in and on the water since I was big enough to toddle."

"That would be swell." He paused and then added formally, "I'm Dave Carter, by the way."

"I'm Peggy Richards."

"I'm glad to know you, Peggy. Do you go to school here?"

"I'll start my second year at U.C.L.A. in September," Peggy told him. "This summer and on the weekends during the school year I work as a waitress at the Green Cove. That's a little seafood restaurant a couple of miles from here. One of about a thousand, I guess."

"You must be an ambitious gal." Dave paused before volunteering his own status. "I just started a job last week. I work in the sporting goods department of Bartell's Department Store."

"Oh?" Peggy looked surprised. "I would never have guessed you to be a salesman. Somehow you look like the college type."

"We can't all be waitresses at the Green Cove!"

Actually, he had given little if any thought to his type or what his choice of a profession would be if he had one to make. It had been enough, after a week of combing newspaper ads and applying at one place after another, to find himself with work of any kind.

He had been at Bartell's for a week now. The first days had been extremely difficult. He had found to his disgust that the mere effort of standing on his feet all day had left him dizzy and exhausted. The act of concentration, simply to add up a bill, had made his head ache. When he returned to the apartment in the evenings, he had fallen across the bed, too nauseated to make the effort to go out to eat.

"You're going to make yourself sick again," Lance had warned him. "There are bound to be easier ways to make a living if you just look around for them."

"Well, if you find one, tell me about it," Dave answered wearily. "I don't notice you out stampeding the employment offices."

"I've got my eyes open. I'll latch onto something before too long."

What Lance did with his time, Dave did not know, for the younger boy volunteered nothing about his activities. He stayed out late in the evenings with the various "friends" who appeared to be nameless, for Dave had yet to meet any of them, and was still in bed in the mornings when Dave left the apartment. During the day he evidently spent a good deal of his time at the beach, for his hair was bleached almost white from the salt and sun, and his clear, flawless skin was a dark, smooth brown. His eyes glowed startlingly green against his tan, and his teeth, when he smiled, seemed an incredible white. His build, though still spare and slender, had thickened through the shoulders and back, and surfer's muscles were beginning to show in his calves and thighs.

In three months' time his body seemed to have begun to change from a boy's build to that of a young man, but the childlike beauty of his face remained the same. It was like a golden mask, beyond which Dave could not seem to reach, no matter how hard he tried.

"Tell me about us," he would ask in a rush of frustration. "What was our family like? How did we live? What did we do? Tell me some of the things that happened when we were little."

"We were just an ordinary family. Nothing special. We didn't do anything every family doesn't do."

"What were our parents like?" Dave persisted. "Our father—what did he look like? Where did he work?"

"He worked in a bank," Lance said. "He was a big man. Tall." He paused and then added, with a burst of unaccustomed feeling, "He was a tryant. He ran everybody. He never let anybody do anything."

Dave regarded him with surprise. "You didn't like him?"

"I hated him," Lance said coldly. "So did you. We were both glad when he died."

"I can't believe that," Dave said in horror. "Our own father!" He hesitated before he asked, "What about our mother—what was she like?"

"Little. Pretty. Kind of soft and weak. She'd believe anything you told her. You could put anything over on Mother." Lance gave his head a shake, as though to clear it of memories. He raised his eyes to Dave's, flashing him a sudden, bright smile.

"They're out of our lives, Dave—way behind us. Why try so hard to remember? What does it matter? We're here now. We have the present, the future. This is God's own country! Why don't you get out in it and enjoy it?"

Now, sprawled on the hot beach, feeling the sun's rays sinking into him, Dave was forced to admit to himself that his brother had been right. Getting outside on weekends was better for him than moping about the apartment, struggling to dredge up memories that refused to come. Slowly his strength and endurance were returning to him; his appetite was coming back. He was able now to go through a workday without crumbling completely in the evening.

Even the headaches, which struck so blindingly, were coming less frequently. Perhaps soon he would really feel up to trying a surfboard!

Across from him, Peggy was gathering herself to rise.

"I guess I'd better get a move on. I've got to get

showered and dressed and to work. It was nice meeting you, Dave."

"It was great talking to you, Peggy."

He turned his gaze to her again. There was something about her that caught at him, a strange feeling that he had known her before, had known her well.

Impulsively, he said, "I'd like to see you again. Would you consider going out with me sometime? To a movie or something?"

"I don't know. I hardly know you." Her gaze was open and guileless.

"If I came over to the Green Cove, could you have dinner with me?"

"Not during working hours." She hesitated. "Maybe if you came late, we could have coffee together. The Cove closes at ten. I'm free after that."

"That would be swell."

He did know her, he was certain. He had met her somewhere, somehow.

He got to his feet and, standing beside her, he was aware of the fact that she was almost as tall as he. Her gray eyes looked directly into his own.

"The Southwest," she said.

"What?" He stared at her, uncomprehending.

"You know, I said you didn't sound like New York, and you asked what you *did* sound like? I know now—it's the Southwest. I hear a lot of people when I'm waiting tables, and I'd guess you to be from Arizona or New Mexico or somewhere like that."

She laughed at the look on his face.

"That's funny, isn't it?"

Nine

It was exactly noon when they drove across the bridge over the Rio Grande into the town of Juarez, Mexico.

The summer heat had reached its midday peak as Frank maneuvered Dan's old Chevrolet along the narrow streets that separated the rows of storefronts, turning the wheel from side to side and coming, every few yards, to a complete stop to avoid the swarms of dogs and dark-skinned children who wandered aimlessly back and forth from one sidewalk to the other.

They had originally planned to start early during the cooler hours of the morning, but there had been one thing after another to detain them—Mr. Drayfus had left for work later than usual because of a cancellation of his first appointment—Eddie had needed to be driven over to a friend's house—Mrs. Cotwell had wanted some things from the grocery store. And then, just as they were preparing to leave the house, the Drayfus phone had rung.

"It's"—Joan had turned to him with a shining face—"it's *Mother!*"

The conversation had not been a long one, but when she replaced the receiver Joan's eyes had been glowing.

"She just wanted to know how we were! The doctors told her she could call us! She wanted to be sure that we were keeping the roses watered, and she asked me to go to the library and pick out some books to bring up to her when we visit Sunday. She says they don't have anything there worth reading, and she's getting awfully tired of television.

"Oh, Frank!" There had been a lilt in her voice that he had not heard there for many months. "She sounded so *normal!*"

Now the happiness lingered in her voice, even though she had to wipe the perspiration from her eyes to read the address on the scrap of paper she held before her:

"This is the right street. Now all we have to do is locate the shop number. It's four twenty-seven—El Mercado."

"That means 'The Market,'" Frank translated ruefully. "Is that supposed to be the name of the shop or what?"

"I think so," Joan said. "Are you familiar with the town, Frank?"

"No. I've only been down here a couple of times. In fact, the last time was about four years ago."

The memory of that last time swept back upon him now, startling him with its many details of recollection. They had come down as a family, and it was in the winter—late November, perhaps, or early December, as the purpose of the trip had been Christmas shopping. Dan had not had his driver's license yet, and Mr. Cotwell had done all the driving. Mrs. Cotwell had carried a list of so many dozens of things she wanted to purchase that they had all laughed at her. And Eddie, who was only eight at the time and inclined to wander, had slipped out of their hands during a stop at one of the stores and turned up an hour later, sitting on the curbing with a group of Mexican children munching a taco.

Dan had had his own shopping to do, and Frank could remember standing beside him, watching as he studied the assortment of turquoise and silver spread out upon the counter of one of the jewelry stores.

"Are you getting Mom's present?" he had asked him, and Dan had smiled and said, "Among others."

He had chosen a curved silver pin, shaped like an orchid, and then, after a slight hesitation, three other pins, smaller and less ornate.

"Who are those for?" Frank had asked him.

"Oh, I thought I might give one to Anne Tonjes. And maybe one to Barbara Johnston. Even if I decide not to, they'll be good to keep on hand. You never know when you might be dating a girl who has a sudden birthday."

"Girls!" Frank gave a snort of disgust.

"Give yourself time, little brother," Dan had said in amusement. "Girls are pretty nice when they reach a certain age. Give yourself a year or so. You'll be buying trinkets too."

How easy it had been for Dan even then. How confident and self-assured he had been! I'm older now than he was then, Frank thought, and I've never had a girl to give anything to. I wonder if Marcie Summers has a bunch of guys who give her things on her birthday.

His mind flew to Marcie, as he had seen her only days ago at the pool. She had been wearing a pink bathing suit, one piece, modestly cut, and her arms and legs had been shining with suntan oil. She had had on a swimming cap when he first caught sight of her, but then she had turned and seen him looking at her, and had quickly reached up to remove it. It was like releasing spun gold from a cage as her long pale hair came springing forth and tumbling over her shoulders.

"You'll never get it back on again."

He had spoken quickly, before his nerve could desert him.

"That's okay. I've had my swim." She had dimpled up at him. "What have you been doing with yourself, Frank? I haven't seen you since school let out."

"Oh, I've been around."

His tongue had frozen then, and he had not been able to move it. What in the world did you say to girls when they just stood there in front of you? What would he say if she were Joan?

Of course, Joan wasn't exactly a girl, she was a *person*. With Joan you could act natural, the way you would with another fellow.

Drawing a deep breath, he forced his tongue into motion.

"If you think you can ever get back into that thing, I'll race you the length of the pool. I might even buy you a Coke when we get there."

When he heard his own voice, his heart had stopped beating. Had he actually spoken those words, or had he merely thought them? He could not have spoken them aloud. He simply couldn't have! This wasn't Joan Drayfus, it was Marcie Summers!

For a moment the slim blond girl had stood there, staring at him. Then, to his complete amazement, she had reached up and begun slowly to replace her swimming cap.

I wish that Dan were here now, Frank thought longingly. I wish I could talk to him about Marcie—about the way I feel when I'm around her. How do you make a girl start to like you? How do you *know* when she *does* like you? Dan . . . darn it, Dan . . .

As it did so often, at odd times, without warning, the sharp pain of loss stabbed through him. He was back four years ago on that happy pre-Christmas sojourn, with the smell and feel of the holidays glowing about him. His mother had bought a huge papier-mâché angel, and Dan, laughing like Santa Claus, had carried it over his shoulder like a toy sack.

"There it is! Over there!" Joan spoke suddenly beside him. "Four twenty-seven! See, Frank—on the corner!"

"Where? That place over there?" Frank came back to the present with a jolt. "That can't be the shop. It looks like somebody's garage."

"It's not though—see the sign? El Mercado—there in red over the doorway." Joan leaned forward. "Look, they've even got a little parking lot."

"That will help, anyway."

Twisting the wheel as far as he could, Frank began to inch the car up the narrow dirt driveway into the parking area at the back of the building.

He locked the car with care, conscious of the curious glances of the crowd of grimy children playing along the edge of the gutter.

Joan was beginning to look worried.

"You're right about this not looking like a jewelry store. Do you suppose I could have got the wrong name and street number?"

"Well, we'll find out," Frank told her. With a last

uncertain glance at the car, he led the way around the corner of the building to the front entrance.

The interior of the shop was poorly lighted and dusty, and a clutter of odd tin lanterns and plastic figures hung in clusters from the low ceiling. Along the walls stood a collection of pots and dishes of assorted colors, many of them chipped so that the clay showed through the shine of the glaze, and beyond them rose a pile of rickety wooden chairs with woven seats, piled one on top of another in a precarious structure that seemed to dare anyone to ask to purchase other than the topmost one.

The rest of the room contained wooden tables piled high with charms and trinkets of the quality usually found in a typical dime store, with prices marked in pesos rather than cents and dollars. There were no customers in the shop, nor did there seem to be a proprietor.

Frank saw on Joan's face a reflection of the same doubt that he knew must show on his own.

"It must be the wrong place," she said in a low voice. "This isn't a jewelry shop, and there's nobody—"

There was a movement against the back wall, and a man emerged from the shadows.

"May I help you, please?"

The English words were spoken with a heavy Spanish accent.

"We're here because—that is, Mr. John Brown from Las Cruces sent us," Joan said uncertainly. "We were to pick up some things for him. I don't know though—I think maybe we've come to the wrong place."

"Mr. Brown from Las Cruces?" The man's eyes

flickered from one face to the other. "May I ask your names, please?"

"I'm Joan Drayfus," Joan said more firmly. "My brother, Larry, used to work for Mr. Brown. This is a friend of mine, Frank Cotwell. He drove me down from Las Cruces."

"You're Larry's sister?" The little eyes regarded her with what seemed to be new interest. "We read about his disappearance in the El Paso paper. A tragic thing. They have never found a trace, have they?"

"No," Joan said shortly.

"Terrible. Terrible. May I offer my sympathy?"

"Thank you."

The man shifted his attention to Frank. "And you, Mr. Cotwell, you were nice enough to drive the young lady? Where, please, have you parked your car?"

"In your lot, behind the shop." Frank was surprised at the question. "It will be safe there, won't it?"

"We will make sure that it is. I will have my boy keep an eye on it. There has been some looting around this neighborhood recently. Once the schools are closed for the summer the children cannot find enough to do for themselves." The man went over to a doorway in the back of the shop and called up a stairway. "José? I have a special customer here. Will you go out to the lot and keep an eye on his automobile?"

He paused, and turned back to Frank.

"The make of the car, please?"

"It's a Chevrolet."

"A Chevrolet, José," he called, and then added a sentence in Spanish.

"Sí, Papa."

The voice that answered was neither a child's nor an adult's; it was a cracked, adolescent voice, much as Frank's own had been the year before. There was the sound of footsteps, and a slight, black-haired boy came hurrying down the stairway. He gave Joan and Frank a quick, curious glance before slipping past them and out through a side door.

"José will keep watch on it. He is a good boy. You will now come with me, please?" The man turned and led the way past the stairway, through a curtain-covered doorway that led into a back room.

The second room, which appeared to be a storeroom of sorts, was as dusty and cluttered as the front one, with boxes and crates piled from one wall to the other. A table at the back held a metal case, and it was to this that the man went. Removing a key from his pocket, he unlocked the case and with great care slid out the inside drawer. From this he withdrew a necklace and a pin.

For a long moment he stood holding them as though loath to let them out of his possession. Then he turned to Joan.

"Would you like to see these before I wrap them?"

"Oh yes," She crossed the room to stand beside him, bending to examine the two pieces on the flattened palm. There was a pause. Then she said, "They're— they're very nice."

"They are beautiful," the man corrected her firmly. "They will be a great item in the States."

Frank's curiosity got the best of him. "Could I see too?"

He moved up until he could see the jewelry over Joan's shoulder. It was silver and turquoise, as most of the Mexican jewelry was. The necklace was of a simple sunburst design. The pin appeared to be a close reproduction of those that Dan had purchased on that shopping trip four years before to give away as birthday gifts.

To Frank's uneducated eyes, there seemed nothing unique about either piece. The silver pin his mother had at home was more graceful and attractive than these.

"I guess I don't know jewelry," he said awkwardly.

"It takes study and knowledge to judge anything properly," the proprietor told him.

The boxing and wrapping of the two small pieces took a quarter of an hour. Standing impatiently in the heat of the windowless room, Frank found it impossible to understand how the mere wrapping and tying of a simple parcel could be so time-consuming. The man wrapped it first in cotton, then in paper, then in a cardboard box, then in paper again. When he had the job completed at last, he excused himself and disappeared up the stairway to what was evidently the living quarters above the shop in search of the designs themselves.

"You'd think he'd have had it all ready for us, wouldn't you?" Joan said in a low voice.

"This whole thing is crazy," Frank said irritably. "What did you think of that jewelry? Is that something every store in New York is going to be howling for?"

"It looked pretty ordinary to me," Joan admitted. "But, then, we don't know about such things. Maybe we see too much silver out here and people in other parts of the country are more impressed with it."

"The original Indian designs are nicer than those," Frank said. "The kind of stuff they peddle on street corners. What is it about those two pieces that makes them special enough for all this intrigue?"

"I don't know any more than you do," Joan said. She reached up a hand and pushed her damp hair back from her forehead. "Don't you suppose we could wait out in the front room as well as in here?"

"I don't see why not." Frank shoved the curtain aside and held it for her to pass through. He could feel the perspiration sliding in rivulets down his neck beneath the light material of his cotton shirt.

As they stepped into the outer room of the shop, the boy, José, was entering through the side door from the parking lot. He slid past them with the agility of an eel and mounted the stairway after his father.

"I thought he was supposed to be out there watching the car," Frank said. "Dan will never forgive me if . . ."

The words faded off and silence fell empty behind them.

When he spoke again, it was almost apologetically.

"I still keep thinking about it as Dan's car. He was so darned proud of it."

"I know. Still"—Joan tried to smile—"it's *your* car now. He would have wanted it to be. And your using it to drive me down here—he would have liked that."

There were footsteps on the stairs, and José's father appeared as suddenly as he had vanished. He was carrying the wrapped parcel and a thick envelope.

"Here you are." He handed them to Joan. "Here, too, is a sales receipt for you to show when you go through customs."

"What," Frank asked, "if the people at customs want to inspect the package?"

"They may do so, of course," the man said easily. "There should be no problem at all. You are taking back only two pieces of jewelry, both priced well below your quota. You will be able to make many such trips before there is any question raised."

"According to Mr. Brown, we should be coming down fairly regularly," Joan said. "Maybe as often as every two weeks. Will there be new designs each time?"

"Mr. Brown, our Las Cruces representative, will inform you as things are ready." After detaining them for so long, now suddenly the man seemed anxious to terminate all conversation. He stepped forward and held the door for them, and a moment later they were plunged into the brilliance of the outside world.

The sun struck blindingly across their faces and a million odors leapt to their nostrils. Their ears were filled with a multitude of sounds—the drone of flies, the shrill yapping of a dog, the shouts and laughter of children, the monotonous chant of street peddlers with their trays of tacos and enchiladas.

Before them on the lot, the car was still safely parked where they had left it, the doors locked, the windows intact.

"I worry too much," Frank said.

"You do, Frank. You really do." Joan reached out and touched the smooth paint of the fender. "See, none of those children have even touched it."

"It's this whole business," Frank said slowly. "I don't understand it. That's the thing, Joan—there doesn't seem to be anything wrong with it, and yet it doesn't make sense. I worry when I don't understand things."

"Well, don't think I'm going to continue with it after I get Larry's debt paid off," Joan said. "I'm glad you came with me today. That man—that whole grubby little shop—gives me the creeps."

They got into the car, and Frank cast a last quick

glance at the second-story window that looked out over the parking lot. He had a faint, uncomfortable feeling that the eyes of José and his father were focused upon them as he turned the key in the ignition and started the engine.

Ten

"Peggy! Peggy, Dave's here!" Mrs. Richards' voice floated up from the downstairs hallway.

"I'll be down in just a minute, Mom! Tell him to wait!"

In the little room at the end of the hall, Peggy Richards began hurriedly to take down her curlers.

Sprawled on one of the twin beds in the room they shared, her fourteen-year-old sister Sarah regarded her with amazement.

"Tell him to wait? You know he's going to wait with the twins down there. They'll be attached to him like weights, one on each knee, and Ginger's probably piggy-back on his shoulders."

"If that's so," Peggy said wryly, "I'll never be able to pry him out of the living room. Those kids act like he's heaven's gift to the Richards family."

"I know somebody else who acts the same way," Sarah said teasingly.

"Don't be so silly."

"When you get up at six o'clock on Sunday morning to wash and set your hair *before* going to the beach, I'd say that was a sign of something."

Peggy shot her sister an irritated glance and dumped a handful of clips into the tray on the dressing table.

The frustrating thing was that Sarah, as usual, was right. It was ridiculous to take pains with your hair when your date was to go swimming. Still, here she was, taking down the curls, relieved to find them falling in the right direction, wondering if Dave would like her bangs curled forward over her forehead instead of pulled back with a band in the way he was used to.

You're an idiot, Peg Richards, she told herself helplessly, letting a boy you hardly know turn you inside out like this. True, you're not exactly a glamor girl, but with classes starting at the college in a couple of weeks, you'll be meeting plenty of nice fellows. There will be proms and football games and fraternity parties, and you'll get asked to them, just the way you were last year. Why do you have to go all soft in the head about some oversized redhead who sells sporting goods in a department store!

She knew as she asked the question that she would have no answer for it, and she reached for a comb, smiling ruefully at her reflection in the mirror before her. From the first moment she had met Dave Carter, sprawled there on that beach towel, the freckles bright against his nose, his eyes squinted against the sun, all the other boys she had ever known had faded into nothing. It had taken her twenty minutes of careful planning before she worked her nerve up enough to walk over to him and ask him the time. It was the first time she had ever done such a thing, and she had worried all the way home that he might think back on it later and decide that she was too forward and never make any effort to call her or look her up at all.

The worry had been unnecessary, for he had turned up at the Green Cove two nights later. She had glanced up from the table she was clearing and had seen him there in the doorway, and relief had washed through her. It had taken her a moment to steady herself enough to cross the room to him and say lightly, "Dave, hello!"

"Hello, miss." He had regarded her with mock seriousness. "I'm looking for a gal in a red swimming suit. Has she been in here tonight?"

"Not that I've noticed," Peggy told him happily, "but if you'll sit down, I'll bring you some coffee, and maybe we can wait for her together."

They had sat over coffee and talked that evening until the manager had finally told them wearily that he had to lock the doors for the night. When she thought back on it, Peggy realized that it was she and not Dave who had done most of the talking. He had sat across from her, smiling and interested, asking questions, laughing at her stories, seeming fascinated by the antics of her big, fatherless family. He had volunteered little, however, about his own background. Even now, after dating him for two months, she knew only that he came from New York and lived at the Royal Palm with his younger brother.

Still, she thought reasonably, it wasn't as though they had spent a lot of time alone together where confidences would come out easily. Their working hours did not coincide, and she was reporting at the Green Cove at almost the same moment Dave was leaving Bartell's. The only time they really had to date was on Sunday, and this was family day at the Richards', with church and beaching and a big midafternoon dinner. From the first moment Dave had walked in the door, he had been absorbed in the turmoil. From Sarah through the eight-year-old twins to five-year-old Ginger, he had been welcomed warmly and enthusiastically as an addition to the family.

"Dave must come from a big family himself," Mrs. Richards had commented one time, "to fit in so well. He seems to really enjoy having the twins climb all over him."

"I think he comes here as much to see the children," Sarah had commented mischievously, "as he does to see Peggy."

For Peggy, the comment had struck home a little too closely for comfort. Although she knew it was ridiculous, it *did* sometimes seem to her that Dave Carter got as much pleasure out of the noisy brood of romping youngsters as he did out of being alone with her. In fact, on the few occasions when they did get out together, it was very often with the twins tagging along behind them and Ginger perched high on Dave's broad shoulders.

Well, not today, she thought now, giving the new curls a final pat and glancing about for a beach robe to pull on over her bathing suit. Today they can beg all they want to, and I'm not going to give in. A date is a date, whether it's to a dance or just to the beach, and the kids have got to learn to respect that.

"See you later," she said briskly to Sarah, and then added, as an afterthought, "You might take a couple of hours and clear some things out from under your bed today. It's shoved so high off the floor now that pretty soon you're going to have to get on and off it with a stepladder."

Despite her firm intentions, getting herself and Dave out of the house without an escort of adoring children proved to be a lengthy and exhausting procedure. It was only after promises to "bring him back for dinner" and "to play Monopoly later" that it was accomplished.

When they were finally out on the sidewalk, headed

for the beach, Dave was still laughing about the fort the twins had under construction in the back yard.

"They've got everything in the world nailed onto it," he said in amusement. "Boards and ladders and old chair backs and tin cans. It'll take a bulldozer to knock the thing down when they're ready to dismantle it."

"Well, that's boys for you!" Peggy laughed with him. "Were you that way too, Dave? Did you build a fort when you were a little boy?"

"I . . . don't know." Suddenly the laughter was gone from his voice. "I guess I must have. All kids do, don't they?"

It was one of those odd moments that occurred so often between them. They could be chatting away easily and happily about almost anything and suddenly there would be some comment, some remark or question, never anything important or even very personal, and the atmosphere would change. She would feel him leave her, not physically, of course, but emotionally; it was like a curtain dropping down behind his eyes, shutting him away from her.

Where are you, she longed to call to him. What are you thinking? I'm here right beside you! Reach out to me! Tell me! Whatever it is, let me share it with you!

The fact that she never did so was, she knew, a mark of cowardice. She was afraid that, if she asked him, she might learn the answer, and that it would be something she would wish afterward she did not know. Another girl, for instance. As attractive as Dave was, there must surely have been a number of girls over the years. Even now, there could easily be others. Just because they spent their Sundays and occasional late after-work hours together, just because he seemed contented and happy in the Richards' home, it didn't mean that he didn't see other girls also. There were all those evenings when she was at work at the Green Cove. Surely he didn't just go back to a one-room apartment and read a book.

And yet, there couldn't be anyone really important, or he would not be with her on Sundays. There was no reason for him to spend his one free day with Peggy Richards if he was truly interested in someone else. No, "the girl," if she existed, couldn't be anyone he had met here in California. She was back in New York, probably—one of those smooth, sophisticated career girls— a society girl with a big city background and enough money to afford all the right clothes and the poise with which to wear them. The kind of girl that somebody like Peggy Richards could never really hope to compete with.

Still, what could this have to do with that chance comment about building a fort? And if Dave was from that kind of background, why was he here in California, working in a department store? Why didn't he have nice clothes himself—she could count on the fingers of one hand the items of clothing that composed the wardrobe he wore when they went out together—and why didn't he have a car? His brother had one, a shabby-looking little Volkswagen. Dave had borrowed it once or twice, but generally they walked where they wanted to go or used the bus. And that brother—he was strange in himself. Or perhaps it was the relationship that was strange. They never seemed to go anyplace or do anything together. As much as Dave seemed to enjoy family life, and with his brother his only relative, why weren't they closer? How could they live together in one room and lead such separate lives that they never even appeared to see each other?

Suddenly, as though he had been reading her thoughts, Dave said, "There's Lance."

"Where?" They had reached the entrance to the public beach now. Although it was early, already the sand was crowded with bright-colored beach towels and gay umbrellas, and people sporting varied degrees of suntan ranging from bright red to almost black swarmed about like a massive colony of two-legged ants.

"There," Dave gestured toward the end of the boardwalk. "The kid in the plaid shorts talking to those two men. The one with the blond hair and the surfboard over his shoulder."

"That's Lance!" Peggy could not keep the astonishment from her voice. "Why, he doesn't look like you at all! I'd never guess you were related!"

"Brothers don't always look alike." There was a defensive note in Dave's voice.

"No, of course not. Still . . ." She stood quietly for a moment, watching the boy with the blond hair. He was listening hard to whatever it was the two men were telling him. There was an intent look on his face as he nodded with understanding, and then suddenly he smiled. It was the bright sweet smile of an angel, and it went straight to her heart.

"He looks like a darling!" Peggy exclaimed. "And he's so young! I didn't realize he was so young, Dave!"

"He's not really. He's just got that kind of a face." Dave poked her teasingly. "Want me to go get him for you? You can take him home and add him to your brood."

"I do think you might bring him over for a meal once in a while. It's not fair for—" She broke off abruptly. The men had turned, and for the first time she saw their faces clearly. "Dave—those people Lance is talking to—how in the world does he happen to know them?"

"Gosh, I don't know." Dave looked surprised. "He makes his own friends. I don't know anything about the guys he runs around with. He meets people at the beach and I guess there's kind of a surfing crowd. Why? Do you know them?"

"I know Jack Wesley," Peggy said, frowning. "He was a couple of years ahead of me in high school. He's bad news, Dave."

"What do you mean?"

"Well, he was wild even in high school, the kind of guy none of the mothers wanted their daughters dating. He never graduated. There was some kind of scandal. It got hushed up, but rumor had it that he was involved in some kind of ring that was peddling dope to students. Since then I know he's been in and out of jail at least once."

"He sure doesn't sound like a very good influence for a kid like Lance," Dave agreed seriously. "Do you know the other guy?"

"No, but I think I've seen him some place. He looks older. I see so many faces at work and here at the beach, it's hard to remember all of them." She paused and then said, more slowly, "In the newspaper?"

"You've seen his picture?"

"I can't remember. I have a feeling I may have. Maybe it will come back to me." She dropped the subject as quickly as she had seized it. "Ready for a swim?"

"Sure! I'll race you to the water!"

He grinned at her, and the curtain was gone, as though it had never fallen between them. They were two healthy young people on a beautiful day with sunshine on their backs and salt wind in their faces, and what shadows could there possibly be except imagined ones!

There's no other girl, Peggy told herself firmly. There can't be! If there were, she would never have let him get away from her!

Laughing at herself and her own silliness, she let the beach robe fall from her shoulders and broke into a run toward the water.

Eleven

The long months of summer moved slowly past, and August became September.

It was autumn in name only, Joan thought, gazing out across the sun-dried lawn to the hollyhocks, dangling wearily from their stalks along the back fence in heat-drenched fatigue. School had started early this year, even before Labor Day, and it seemed strange to see children still in shorts and sun dresses toting their books and pencil boxes along the sidewalks in the mornings and home again in the heavy heat of midafternoon.

"The hottest summer in thirty years," the weather bureau called it. Besides this, it was the driest. State rainfall was at a minimum, and a fire broke out in the Gila Wilderness Area, raging for almost a week before it was finally subdued by emergency fire-fighting units borrowed from the Indian reservations. After this, all national parks and forests were closed to campers.

The rivers that had roared through the Mogollons in the spring dwindled to sluggish creeks. For a brief time the search was renewed for the "bodies of two Las Cruces boys, Daniel Cotwell and Lawrence Drayfus, Jr., lost in the Wilderness Area the end of April." But even though the rivers were now shallow, no traces of the boys were found.

The newspaper articles that accompanied the new search were repetitions of those that had run previously. They reviewed the boys' backgrounds, the fact that Dan had been an honor student and captain of the high school football team, the news that Larry had been accepted by one of the state's top military academies and was to have begun classes there in the fall. They described the canteen, identified as Dan's, which had been found on the bank of the river.

"The families still hope," one article said, and Joan read it with a flash of anger.

"How can they say such a stupid thing!" she exclaimed to her father. "How can the families possibly hope after this long! There can't be any hope. We know that and have accepted it."

"Newspapers just look for things to say to fill up their columns," Mr. Drayfus said soothingly. "Actually, the end of hope is a good thing. Your mother's proved that."

Joan nodded, light returning to her face.

"Oh, Daddy, won't it be wonderful to have her home again!"

"It certainly will," Mr. Drayfus said quietly. "It's been a long summer for all of us."

On their last visit to the sanitarium, Mrs. Drayfus had voluntarily talked to them about Larry. It was the first time she had mentioned him since the day of her breakdown.

"He is dead." She spoke the words slowly and deliberately. "I know that now. I've known it, really, I think, all along, but I wasn't able to accept it. It was as though by refusing to admit the fact, I was keeping it from being real.

"The doctors here have helped me to realize that I

can't spend the rest of my life dwelling on Larry. I have memories of him, and they are happy ones. He was a wonderful boy—sweet and fine and good—a son to be proud of. He only had seventeen years of life, but they were happy years, filled with love. Think of the mothers who lose their children and don't have this knowledge to sustain them."

"He would have been a fine man," Mr. Drayfus agreed. "Whatever misunderstandings he and I had, I never doubted that fact for a minute. I loved him too, Margaret, deeply and strongly. Can you believe that now?"

Mrs. Drayfus smiled a little shakily.

"I never *didn't* believe it, Lawrence. I was just so busy agonizing over my own grief that I wouldn't let myself acknowledge anyone else's. Of course, you loved him— we all loved him. And he loved us. We were a close, happy family, and the memory of that will be something we'll share always.

"But, now"—she made an effort to steady the smile and blink back the tears that filled her eyes—"Larry's gone, and we've still got a lot of life ahead of us. And we're still a family. I have a fine husband and a wonderful daughter. I guess that makes me a pretty lucky woman."

"It's we who are lucky," Mr. Drayfus said quietly. "We were afraid we had lost you as well as Larry. Thank God—oh, Margaret, thank God we're going to have you back again!"

The doctor, when they talked with him afterward, had told them that, if she continued improving as steadily as she was, Mrs. Drayfus would be ready to come home in October.

"Of course, we can't expect miracles," he said warn-

124

ingly. "This is not a strong woman and she probably never will be. She has made remarkable recovery this summer, but that doesn't mean that she has turned into an emotional mountain. She has led a very protected existence here at the sanitarium. Coming home will not be easy for her."

"Do you think"—Mr. Drayfus looked worried—"that it will be *too* difficult for her? Are we rushing things? Would it be better to postpone the homecoming a little while longer?"

The doctor shook his head. "I can't see that there would be anything to be gained by that. The adjustment will have to be made sometime, and probably the sooner it is started, the better. Protect her as much as you can —make home life easy and pleasant. Speak naturally about your son and recall the happy memories you have of him. Show her you love and need her. She'll make it all right."

They carried the encouraging words back with them and repeated them often to each other:

"Show her you love and need her—she'll make it . . ."

"And I'll be home," Joan added. "That should make a difference. It won't be as though she'll be here alone in the house."

"You're sure you don't mind too much, Joanie?" The old frown of worry fell into its familiar creases in her father's forehead. "It can't be easy having all your friends going off to college without you. I know how long you've planned on attending the university. You and Dan used to talk about it so much."

"It doesn't matter now the way it used to," Joan told him truthfully. "So much has happened that things are in a different perspective. It doesn't seem important to go to college just because everybody else is doing it. Oh, I still want to go," she added quickly. "And I *will* go. I still want to become a teacher. But whether it's this year or next or even the year after that doesn't matter. Not if I'm needed here."

"You've grown up this year, daughter." Her father smiled at her affectionately. It was a tired smile. Joan noticed, as she watched it, the new lines in his face and the deepening of the gray at his temples.

"Maybe," he added with a touch of wryness, "we all have."

Despite her brave words, however, Joan had a struggle with self-pity when Anne Tonjes came to say goodbye on her way to the airport. The sight of the car filled with luggage and Anne's bright fall suit ("I'll swelter in it!" she admitted, "but I'm darned if I'm going to arrive at U.C.L.A. looking like I'm fresh off the mesa!") brought back with a rush the excited plans they had made together the summer before.

"You'll come out for a visit, won't you?" Anne asked, giving her a hard hug. "For a football weekend or something? I'll dig you up a dreamboat for a date, I promise!"

Joan laughed despite herself. "Here she is, not even on campus yet—she doesn't know a soul—she doesn't even have a date of her own, but she's offering me Rock Hudson!"

"Well, we might as well aim high!" There was a note of seriousness beneath the laughter. "You *will* come, won't you, Joanie? Just for a few days before your mother gets home? The change of scene will do you good, and a few dates with college men won't hurt you any either. You can't spend the rest of your life as a recluse because of Dan."

"Oh, I don't intend to," Joan assured her. "If somebody nice comes along, I'll be glad to date him. I can't imagine right now falling in love again, but I suppose even that will happen eventually. Dan was—*Dan*—there can't be anyone like him. But I know there will be other people I'll care about in other ways."

Still, she kept Dan's picture on the table by her bed. She knew that some people would consider this morbid and she was a little guilty about it. When her mother returned, she vowed, she would remove the picture from its frame and place it in her scrapbook as the memory it was. For the time being, however, she left it there. Strangely enough, she did not find it depressing. Just the thought of Dan was a happy thing, and it was much less difficult to sleep at night with the knowledge that a strong face and steady blue eyes were standing guard over her dreams.

She and Frank had made the trip to Mexico four times since the first of what they now termed their "jewelry runs" in early July. Each trip was identical to the first one with the same long wait while the jewelry was packaged and the same envelope of papers containing the designs.

From the first there had been no difficulty about passing through customs. They gave their names and places of birth and the customs officials gave a quick glance at the receipt they offered. One time they had been asked to unwrap the package, and they were always asked if they had anything other than this to declare—pottery, furniture, liquor, clothing. Except for one occasion, when they stopped on the far side of the border to pick up some Mexican slippers as a present for Mrs. Drayfus, their answers were a consistent "No."

Back in Las Cruces they delivered the jewelry to

Mr. Brown at his room at a motel called the Tumble-weed. This too was usually a lengthy procedure, as they were expected to wait while he inspected the jewelry and designs in detail and then wrote them out a receipt in return for their safe delivery.

Looking at him now, at the thin, almost delicate face behind the metal-rimmed glasses, Joan wondered how she could ever have found John Brown a frightening figure. He was a little man, always perfectly dressed, with a brisk, businesslike manner and a politeness that even Frank could not find fault with.

"You can see, I'm perfectly safe," Joan assured him after the second of their trips. "Nobody's going to harm me. All they care about is this delivery. And I know my way now. You don't have to come with me every time."

"I don't want you going down there alone," Frank answered stubbornly.

"Why?" Joan asked curiously. "What are you afraid might happen?"

"That's just it—I don't know. Like I've said since the beginning, I don't understand any of it. I just know I don't like it. I don't like Mr. Brown, I don't like the guy at El Mercado, I don't like that skinny kid José. And Dan wouldn't like them either."

"Frank . . . Frank . . ." Joan shook her head in affectionate exasperation. "You're the worst worrywart I've ever known. But thank you for wanting to come. For . . . everything."

With the start of school in September, it became more difficult to keep the "jewelry runs" concealed from her father. Before then the four-hour round trip could easily be staged during the course of a weekday while Mr. Drayfus was at the office. Now, however, Frank did not

128

get out of classes until three-thirty and some reason had to be offered for her absence from the home when Mr. Drayfus returned home in the evenings.

"I won't lie to him," Joan insisted. "I can't tell him the whole truth, but I won't lie to him either."

She settled finally on simply saying she was "out with Frank," and her father accepted it, as he always did her statements, with a complete faith that left her feeling like a criminal.

"He's a little young for you, isn't he, daughter?" he asked. "He seems like a nice lad, and he certainly resembles Dan, but you can't replace one person with another, you know. Don't you think you might do better to look for somebody entirely new? Maybe go visit Anne the way she suggested? That sort of thing?"

"Oh, Daddy, Frank's just a good friend," Joan told him quickly. "He *is* much too young for me in any romantic way. Besides, he has a girl friend, or at least he's right on the edge of having one. One of the girls in his class, Marcie Summers, has invited him to be her date at a Sadie Hawkins Day hop next weekend."

"I wish you *would* find somebody to be interested in in 'a romantic way,' Joanie," Mr. Drayfus said worriedly. "You used to go out so much. I hate to see you sitting around the house all the time."

"All in good time, Daddy. You can't rush these things." She answered him lightly, but she knew in her heart that he was right. She was spending too much time brooding. With all her high school friends from the year before working at jobs or off at college or, in the case of the boys, in the service, she was finding the long days dull and lonely. Keeping house and cooking for only herself and her father took very little time and effort, and only so many hours a day could be spent in sewing and reading.

I know what I ought to be doing, she admitted to herself grimly, and I keep putting it off because I don't want to face it.

Larry's room still stood with its doors closed, just as she had left it the day she had made the search there for the missing money. His things were there, she knew, in the same neat piles in which she had left them, in which Larry himself had left them almost five months before. Her mother must not be allowed to come home and find them there.

If she thought about it too long or in too much detail, she knew that she would not be able to do it. One bright morning, when the first faint breath of autumn lifted the heat from the air, she armed herself with half a dozen cardboard boxes and went into the room and began lifting piles of clothing out of the bureau.

She started with the top drawer first, the pajamas and socks and underwear. The second drawer contained the shirts, the third the sweaters. She lifted them by the arm-load and dropped them into the boxes, trying not to think too much about what she was doing.

Somebody will wear them, she thought, and be grateful for them. Somewhere there's a family that can't afford nice clothes with a boy who will think it's heaven to have these shirts and sweaters. Larry wouldn't want his things to sit here rotting in the drawers. He would want this boy to have them.

But, would he really? The question nagged irritatingly at the corner of her mind. Larry had always been so possessive about his belongings, particularly his clothing. She could remember the time she had come into his room without his permission and borrowed an old shirt of his to wear to a "shipwreck party." She had come home that night to find him waiting up for her in a state of absolute fury.

"My clothes are *mine,* do you hear me?" he had told her angrily, all but wrenching the shirt off her shoulders. "If you want things, you buy them for yourself!"

"I'm sorry. I didn't think you'd mind." She had been honestly bewildered. "I couldn't find you to ask, and it was an old thing. You never wear it."

"Whether I wear it or not has nothing to do with it," Larry had informed her coldly. "What does matter is that it belongs to me."

Now she hesitated, the memory of the conversation coming back to her. It was silly, she knew, to let such a thing bother her. Larry was dead. He would not have expected his things to be kept as a kind of shrine to his memory. It was not as though he would ever be back to claim them or to use them again.

Still, there were a few things that had been special favorites, several items of clothing that he had cherished and been especially proud of. These things, perhaps, she should keep, put aside in a special box, store somewhere. It was not a reasonable thing to do, but reason and emotion did not always go together. The green ski sweater, for instance, that had been imported from Switzerland—Larry had spent all his earnings from his short-lived paper route on that sweater. It was hard to imagine anyone else wearing it. It had been the exact color of Larry's eyes.

Leaning over the box, she began to thumb through the pile of discarded clothing. There were a number of sweaters and shirts, even the old one from the "shipwreck party." The green sweater was not among them.

That's crazy, Joan told herself. It has to be there. Could I have missed it?

She went through the pile again.

Where could it have vanished? It was like living all over again the unsuccessful search for the money. Things did not just pick themselves up and take themselves off. Larry would not have lent the sweater, not the way he felt about his possessions. Was it possible that he could have taken it on the camping trip with him? It hardly seemed likely. The sweater was much too good and too expensive for knock-about wear. Could it be some place other than the sweater drawer? Perhaps he had kept it on a padded hanger in the closet.

Straightening from her stance over the box, Joan went over to the closet and opened the door. A faint musty smell told her that the clothing needed airing. She reached in a hand and began to slide the hangers along the pole, surprised at the number that were empty. The green sweater was not there, but surely there had been more shirts than this, more pairs of slacks! What about the tan sports jacket? Larry had been so pleased with it. He had purchased it early in the spring. He had been waiting eagerly for the weather to become warm enough for him to wear it.

And the shoes! The shoe bag hung neatly on the back of the door. There were so very many empty compartments. Had they been empty when she was searching the room three months ago? Yes, they must have been, for she could remember feeling into them. It had not occurred to her then to wonder at how few of the compartments had shoes in them.

What in the world has happened to everything!

She turned slowly from the closet to meet the eyes of the portrait on the bureau. The innocent, boy-child's face dimpled at her from within the confines of the walnut frame. The eyes laughed into hers, guileless and gay.

"It's impossible," Joan said softly to her brother's face. "What I was thinking for a minute there—it's completely impossible. I'm ashamed of even thinking it. There has to be some other answer."

Still, she stood for a long moment staring at the photograph. Then abruptly she turned and began pulling clothing from the closet hangers. She worked grimly and hurriedly as though afraid someone would walk in and find her there. She yanked them down recklessly, ignoring the snap of buttons, hurling shirts and slacks and suits alike into the cartons with no attempt at neatness.

"It's impossible," she said again, "but it's the kind of impossible thing that can really get a hold on you. It's the kind of impossible thing that must never—ever —be allowed to occur to Mother."

Twelve

They drove home through the sunset.

It was the time of day Joan liked best, when the desert fell away, shadowy and mysterious on either side of the car. To the west the mountains stood out like purple velvet against the brilliant flame of the sky. The heat of the summer had lifted now; the twilight was cool, and darkness came earlier.

"The coach says by November we'll be practicing under lights," Frank said.

There was a new deep note to his voice, which Joan could not help smiling at hearing. Trying out and making the football team was the shining glory of Frank's life.

"I thought at first they wanted me because of Dan," he had confided when the team was announced. "Being his brother and all, like a sort of legacy. But it's not like that at all. I don't even play the same position. The coach says I'm faster than Dan was. He wants me for quarterback."

"That's wonderful," Joan had told him sincerely. Still, she had gone only once to see him play. The sight of the football field, the shouts of the crowd, the smell of popcorn and candied apples, and it had all come rushing back to her—the dozens of nights she had sat on these same bleachers, tense and excited, leaning forward, straining for the sight of one special figure, square and strong, a little bigger than the others, running in a special way.

She had lived it again in a flash when Frank came running onto the field. She knew him at once without even looking at his number. The way he ran, the way he carried himself—exactly like his brother. The coach was right, he was fast. Even to her untrained eye he seemed to have an ease of motion, a natural, effortless sense of timing. Dan had had it too, to a degree, but not quite to this extent. With Dan, it had been his strength rather than his speed that had brought acclaim.

"Cotwell! Cotwell has the ball!"

Someone behind her yelled it. Then suddenly the whole crowd was on its feet shouting.

"Cotwell! Cotwell!"

"I know him," the girl behind Joan said proudly. "He's in my algebra class!"

"Oh, Dan . . . Dan . . . Joan's eyes stung with tears. She was happy for Frank. Of course, she was. Frank was as dear to her now as a younger brother, closer by far, in fact, than the brother she had lost. It was marvelous that Frank should find himself in this way, should begin receiving recognition for his skills and abilities. And yet, the running figure on the field before her—the beloved, familiar name rising all about her in hundreds of different voices—was for the moment more than she could bear.

Blinking back the tears that would not stop coming, she left her place in the bleachers and walked as quickly as she could toward the parking lot. She did not return.

Now, turning her head to watch Frank's profile

against the sunset, she said, "You were sweet to skip practice today. I know what it means to you to do that. Did the coach say anything?"

"Not much. It's the first time I've missed. He knows I'm reliable." Frank's eyes were on the road ahead. "Say, Joan, how long are we going to keep on with this?"

"You mean our 'jewelry runs'?" Joan shook her head. "I don't know. As long as it takes to pay back Larry's debt, I guess. Mr. Brown hasn't said anything about how long he's going to need us."

"Have you thought about trying to pay it off in some other way?" Frank asked her. "Coming through customs this time, I felt like they were looking us over in kind of a funny way. I don't mean that anything was wrong. We were well below our quota, just like we always are. But the fact that we've made so many trips back and forth lately—they keep records, you know. I think they're beginning to wonder about us."

"Let them wonder. It can't hurt anything. As you say, we're not doing anything wrong." Joan hesitated. "We're *not,* are we, Frank? You're not beginning to feel funny about this, are you?"

"I've always felt funny about it," Frank said bluntly. "I've never liked it, not from the beginning, and I feel a little more uncomfortable about it each time we go down. I can't accept that Mr. Brown as simply a sharp businessman the way you seem to be able to. I don't think he's letting you work off that missing money in this way because of kindness. I think there's a snag somewhere in this, and one of these times we're going to hit it. Nothing as hush-hush as this can be on the up-and-up."

"What do you expect me to do?" Joan asked him. "I

don't really like it either, but what choice is there? I can't go out and take a full-time job, not with Mother coming home in a couple of weeks. If I don't repay the money this way, I won't be able to at all."

"What I think you should do," Frank said, "is tell your father."

"Frank, I can't! You know Daddy has a heart condition. He's had enough to upset him this summer without my adding this one more thing to it!"

"This 'one more thing' is going to look like absolutely nothing compared to everything else that has happened." There was a note of firmness in Frank's voice that made him sound more like a man than a boy. "Your dad has been through all kinds of hell this summer—agreed. But he's held up under it! There are people who are made like that, Joan. They can take the big things and roll with the punches. It's the grind of little everyday pressures that collapses them. I think your dad's that kind of guy.

"Besides, why should this be such a major blow to him? Nobody's accusing Larry of robbing a bank or anything. So he had a job—so he was trusted with some money—so, when he died, his sister couldn't locate it. Your dad makes a good living. He can replace the cash a heck of a lot better than you can."

"It's not *just* replacing the money." Joan spoke slowly. "There's something else."

"You mean there's something you haven't told me?" He turned to her accusingly. "Is there something you've been keeping from me, Joan?"

"No. That is—there wasn't in the beginning. It was just the other day that I . . ." She did not continue.

"Okay, shoot! What happened the other day?"

"Nothing, really. Just an odd thing that made me

think of something for a minute. It couldn't be true. I know that, I *know* it. But, if my parents ever thought of it—I don't know what it might do to them. It's so crazy." She could see his growing impatience. "The thing is, I was going through Larry's clothes, putting them into boxes for storage and to give away. They weren't all there."

Frank was silent a moment as though waiting for her to continue. Finally he said, "So?"

"That's all. Just that they weren't there. There were things missing—a favorite sweater, a new sports jacket. Shirts and things. Some shoes."

"I don't see . . ." He paused as the significance of the statement began to become clear to him. "No guy would take a sports jacket with him on a camping trip."

"No," Joan said, "he wouldn't. Or a good ski sweater. Or suede shoes."

"You can't mean that you think . . ." Now it was he who could not complete the sentence.

"The thing that occurred to me," Joan said with effort, "was that he might not have gone on the camping trip at all. He left the house as though he were going, and then on Sunday, while we were all at church, he came back and packed up some things. He took the money he was holding for Mr. Brown. He just picked up and—and went away!"

"And left you all thinking he was dead!"

"That's why I said, it's so crazy. It couldn't be true. Larry wouldn't do that, he couldn't! *Nobody* could! Nobody could be so cruel to people who love him! It was just something that came into my mind—I was ashamed of it right away. But, still, it *did* come into my mind. And it might—into other people's."

"You mean your parents'?" Frank's hands were

clenched tightly upon the wheel; his knuckles stood out hard and white in the fading light. "I don't think it would, Joan. No parents could believe that about a child of theirs. Besides, like you say, it couldn't be true. I'm not saying that from what I knew of Larry, because I didn't actually know him at all. For all I know, he could have been a sort of monster. But I did know Dan! And Dan was with him!"

"Of course. That shows how silly I was being. Dan would never have gone along with such a thing!" She let her breath out in relief at the simple statement. "There has to be some other explanation for the missing clothes."

"Perhaps he sold them or gave them away or took them to be cleaned. Maybe he packed them up for the summer and you'll run across them in a suitcase some place." Frank offered his explanations with machine-gun intensity. "There are all kinds of things that could have happened to them. Trust a girl to come up with the one that's completely impossible!"

"You're right. That's my excuse—my sex." Joan laughed a trifle giddily. "Imagine, building an idea like that out of nothing! And you're right about telling Daddy. I should have done that in the beginning. I was upset—I guess none of us were really thinking clearly right then. Mother isn't home yet. She won't have to know anything about it."

"Great! No more 'jewelry runs!' I'll be able to make all the practice sessions!" Frank took his foot off the accelerator. "Say, does the car feel kind of funny to you? Like it's pulling to one side?"

"I hadn't noticed, but now that you mention it . . ." Joan frowned. "What do you think is the matter?"

"Probably a flat. We ran over a board or something back there a way. It might have had a nail in it."

He let the car slow itself down, and then, turning the wheel carefully, brought it to a full stop on the shoulder of the road.

Opening the door and throwing a quick glance up and down the highway, Frank climbed out of the car. Sitting quietly in the front seat, Joan watched him walk around to the back. The sky had faded now, and the first pale stars were beginning to show through the gathering darkness. On the road far ahead a strange golden halo announced the approaching awakening of a full moon.

"It's a flat, all right," Frank announced. "It's about the shape of a pancake. No wonder the thing was lurching like that. If we hadn't been so busy talking I would have noticed it right away."

"Oh, dear." Joan opened her own door and got out to stand beside him. "Thank goodness you're here! I bet it's twenty miles to the nearest filling station."

"And you thought you could just as easily start making these trips yourself!" There was a note of real satisfaction in his voice. "Girls! What's the matter with them!"

"Don't forget that Marcie Summers is a girl," Joan said teasingly.

"Yeah. I guess that's what makes her so fascinating —she's just as nuts as the rest of you!"

The cool, sweet air of evening lifted their hair and brushed their faces. Off to either side there was the faint sound of desert things, waking and stirring and coming to life in the welcomed darkness.

Frank muttered under his breath as he opened the trunk and got out the jack and spare tire.

"I sure hope Dan got around to getting this thing patched after the last nail that went through it!"

Joan's eyes found the line of moon gold along the horizon.

"Look," she breathed. "Did you ever see anything so beautiful!" She paused, and when he did not answer she said, "Frank?"

There was still no response. Surprised, she walked around to stand behind him. He had the car up on the jack now and was kneeling beside it. The tire was off, but his attention was not on this, but on something he was holding in his hand.

Joan bent nearer.

"What is it?"

"Darned if I know. It was inside the hubcap." He turned the object in his hands. "Go look in the dashboard compartment and get the flashlight."

She found it immediately and returned to turn the bright beam full upon him. The thing in his hands was a neatly wrapped brown paper parcel.

"It was inside the hubcap?" Joan exclaimed. "How could it have gotten there? Dan wouldn't have had anything there, would he?"

"I can't imagine it." Frank was working with the string. He got the knot untied and gave the brown paper a hard jerk. It came loose and fell aside to disclose a second bag, this one of transparent plastic.

"Well, what do you know!" Frank's voice was hard but unsurprised. "This explains a lot of things. In fact, I guess it explains everything."

He got slowly to his feet, holding the bag straight out in front of him as though he were holding gun powder. Automatically, Joan took a step backward.

"What is it?" she asked nervously.

"What do you think it is? Take a good look." He thrust it out to her. "Don't be scared, it's not going to explode. It's got other uses."

"It looks," Joan said tentatively, "like some kind of dried grass or something. Seeds and stems and things. What is something like that doing in the hubcap?"

"José put it there," Frank said. "It couldn't have been easier. He had plenty of time while we were inside the shop with his father. I'll be willing to bet there's a package just like it in each of the other caps. It's the real reason we've been going back and forth to Mexico."

"The real reason?" Joan repeated in bewilderment. "But what about the designs and the jewelry? What about Mr. Brown's business?"

"We've been helping Mr. Brown's business, all right," Frank said quietly. "It's just a different business than we thought it was. We haven't been making 'jewelry runs' when we brought that junky silver back from Juarez, Joanie. What we've been doing is smuggling in marijuana!"

Thirteen

It was a quarter to ten when Dave Carter arrived at the Green Cove and took a seat at his usual small table by the door.

A pug-nosed waitress who was clearing a nearby table threw him a quick smile of recognition and said, "I'll tell Peggy you're here. She's back in the kitchen. We're running late tonight. A whole batch of people came in just under the wire."

"That's okay," Dave told her. "I don't mind waiting. Just bring me a cup of coffee when you get a chance, and how about a piece of lemon pie?"

"We aren't supposed to take any more orders, but considering you're such a steady customer . . ." The girl gathered up her tray and hurried off in the direction of the kitchen.

A moment later Peggy stuck her head around the edge of the kitchen door and gave him a smile and a wave. Dave raised his own hand in a gesture of greeting, and the head disappeared again.

It was a funny way of dating, to start an evening at ten o'clock, but they had a funny setup anyway, with their hours running the way they did. Now that classes had started at the college, Peggy worked only on weekends, but her weekday nights were reserved for studying.

Fridays and Saturdays, Dave would drop by the Green Cove just before closing time, and they would take in a late movie or walk back to the Richards' house and watch television. On Sundays they went to the beach, often with the mob of younger children in tow, and as often as not Mrs. Richards invited him to stay for mid-day dinner.

"This isn't very fair to you," he had told Peggy more than once. "You've got so little free time, with both school and working, that I shouldn't be taking up so much of it. It doesn't leave you any chance to do anything else."

"Like what?" She had regarded him with surprise. "What else do you think I ought to be doing?"

"Well, there are bound to be things at the college, parties and dances and ball games. There must be plenty of nice guys there who would give their eyeteeth to take you to them."

"Are you telling me you'd like me to date other people?" Peggy had asked him.

"Well, sure, if you want to. I'm not God's gift to young women, Peg, and I know it. I don't have clothes or cash to spend on mad evenings or even a car to get you places. Everything I earn at the store goes to pay for our crummy room and feed Lance and me. I'd be a dope to expect a girl to be happy with that."

"Well, be a dope then," Peggy had said. "Because I am."

She said it flatly, without coyness, giving him that wide, honest look of hers that made him feel that he had known her forever.

"If I wanted to date other people, I would. But I don't."

It was she who had wanted it that way, but still he

144

could not help but feel guilty about it. He was fond of Peggy; in fact, she was the only real friend he had other than a few associates at work. Her big, comfortable house, filled with noise and laughter, was more home to him than the room he and Lance shared at the Royal Palm. Her family—her easygoing, energetic mother—the happy, squabbling brood of brothers and sisters—fed a hunger within him which he could not begin to explain.

Still, he was bothered by the feeling that he was taking more than he was giving in their relationship. As much as he liked Peggy and enjoyed her company, there was something missing in the way he felt about her. He wondered if she was aware of it. Sometimes he hoped she was; it would make it so much easier not to hurt her.

The pug-nosed waitress set his pie and coffee before him.

"Always lemon," she said. "My goodness, you'd think there weren't any other kinds."

"Why settle for second best? When I find a good thing, I stick with it." Belatedly he realized that she would be rushing back to repeat his remark to Peggy. "I *like* lemon," he said more stiffly.

"I like apple, myself," the waitress said conversationally.

I'm getting too sensitive, Dave thought with disgust as the back of the white uniform crossed the room to a far table. Here I am, thinking my every comment is going to get blown up and made into something it isn't. What makes me think Peggy gives a darn about whether I care about her romantically? She probably likes me just the way I do her, as a good friend. Who knows, she may be worrying about being unfair to *me!*

The thought made him feel better. He took a bite of the pie, leaned back in his chair, and let his eyes roam idly about the room. He had been here so often now that he was beginning to feel the affection of familiarity. It was a nice little restaurant, not lavish, but clean and charming. The walls were hung with fishnets and seascapes, and the soft green lights that hung from the ceiling were shaped like blowfish.

Because of the lateness of the hour, there were very few customers left in the dining room. One of the few remaining couples were getting up to leave. At the far table, a group of four, who appeared to be college students, were dawdling over their coffee. Glancing idly in their direction, Dave was surprised to find one of their number, a pretty dark-haired girl, staring at him intently.

There was a familiar look about her, and yet, it was easy to think that all pretty girls looked familiar. Lately he had begun to find himself responding to all sorts of strange things. He would hear a strain of music floating from a jukebox—someone would pass him on the street, walking with a certain stride—the scent of carnations would reach out to him from the open door of a flower shop, and something in his mind would flicker, a spark, flaring bright for only an instant and dying just as quickly before it could catch and flame.

Only a few days ago he had seen three boys coming along the street. They were dressed in jeans and T-shirts, their faces and arms sunburned, and they had evidently just come up from the pier, for they were laughing and kidding each other about "all those fish that got away." The two older boys were talking to each other across the third one's bristly head, and he kept bobbing between them, trying to get into the conversation.

Just as they drew opposite Dave, the oldest boy reached down and rumpled the hair of the small one and said, "Okay, peanut, tomorrow we'll use you for bait and we'll really come home with a catch!"

There was such teasing affection in the voice that Dave, turning to watch them, had found himself smiling in sympathy. Little brothers were a bother, but there was something about them that got you. Lance could never have been that much smaller than he. How then did he know the feeling, the warm surge of almost paternal affection, that a freckled-nosed little brother could call forth? There were only a couple of years between Lance and himself, not the seven or eight that must exist between these boys.

That night, when Lance got home, late as usual, Dave turned over in his bed and asked, "Say, did we ever have a brother?"

The other boy was silent a moment, standing frozen in the moonlight that flowed through the French doors. When he spoke there was an odd note in his voice.

"A brother? What do you mean?"

"I mean, a kid brother. Was it always just the two of us? There wasn't a third one?"

"Nope. Just us." Lance did not move. "Why do you ask?"

"I don't know, really. I saw some kids today, and I seemed to feel—oh, something. Like remembering. But not really. It was just a feeling, like I'd been around a kid brother sometime and I knew how it felt. And then, the way I feel with Peggy's brothers, the twins—I'm *used* to them. I was used to them the first time I met

147

them. It's crazy, I guess. Like I say, I don't actually remember anything. It's just a feeling."

"There used to be a family next door," Lance said slowly, "with a batch of kids. They were always tagging around after us. Maybe that's what you remember."

"Maybe so." He leaned back against the pillows, exhausted at the effort it had taken to drag upon his memory, yet exhilarated as well. "Perhaps this was a first step," he said hopefully. "Maybe it's starting to come back."

"Maybe," Lance said. He did not turn away. "Look, Dave, you keep telling me these things. I mean, if you think you're starting to remember something, you come out with it. Don't just keep it to yourself."

"Okay. I will."

"There isn't anything else, is there? No more 'feelings'?"

"Nope. Just that."

It was so little, but it had been something. And every flicker, every faint crack of light that flashed, even momentarily, through the dark curtain that hung over his mind, was hopeful and exciting.

Now he glanced up and saw Peggy crossing the room toward him. She had changed from her uniform into a skirt and sweater. With her hair fixed that new way, curling forward over her forehead, she might have been a high school girl rather than a working waitress and a college student.

"Hi," she said. "I'm sorry to have been so long. Mary's offered to take over for me now, so I'm free as a bird at last!"

"That's okay. I've been stuffing myself on pie. What do you want to do tonight?" He got to his feet and picked up the bill for the pie and coffee. "We might be able to catch the last feature at the Palm. I think they've got that new comedy playing."

"Sounds fine to me," Peggy said agreeably.

At the cashier's desk she fastened the top button of her sweater while Dave counted out his change. Before them, the college boys from the far table were paying their own bill. Their dates stood apart, over by the door, chatting together. Suddenly the small, pretty one said, "Dan?"

Automatically, Dave raised his head and swung it in her direction. She was staring at him, as she had been earlier from the other table, but now her face was dead white. She looked as though she had just seen a ghost.

"You *are* Dan. You're *Dan Cotwell*."

"I'm sorry," Dave said, "you must have me mixed up with somebody else."

"I don't! I couldn't!" The dark eyes were huge in the small face. "You are Dan, you must be! Nobody could look so much like Dan! Even your voice—the way you walk!"

"I'm sorry," Dave said again. "You're mistaken." He laid the money for the bill on the counter and took Peggy's arm. "Come on," he said hoarsely, "let's get out of here."

They stepped through the door out onto the sidewalk, and the fresh salt breeze swept into their faces. Behind them, the girl and her escort were also emerging from the restaurant, but he did not turn to look back at them. He could feel the girl's eyes on his back; he knew she was staring. He could see in his mind's eye the shock on her face, could hear again the sound of her voice: "Dan!"

She had called him "Dan." He had turned, hearing

the name. He had *reacted* to the name, almost as though it were his own!

What's wrong with me, he asked himself wildly. Am I nuts or something? My name is *David, David Carter!*

He thought, I need a doctor! I've got to see a doctor! No matter what Lance says, something is wrong with me, something more than just a jolt to my mind! I can't go on like this any longer! What if I'm actually crazy! What if all these dark churning things within me should come surging out one day, all these things I don't even know are there, and I turn into a raving maniac or something! What if I hurt somebody!

"Dave!" Peggy's voice was thin and frantic. "Dave, wait, please! I can't keep up with you!"

"I'm sorry." He had forgotten for the moment that she was beside him. He slowed his pace, and realized that his hand was clamped upon her arm. Abruptly he released it.

"I'm sorry," he said again. "We're going to the movies, aren't we? Let's see—which direction—"

"I don't want to see a movie," Peggy said shakily. "I want to talk, Dave! I want to know what's wrong! There's something terribly wrong or you wouldn't be acting like this!"

"No. That is, there's nothing you can do about it."

"That girl back there, she spoke to you! I didn't hear what she said, but you knew her!"

"No. No, I didn't know her," Dave said violently. "I've never seen her before in my life."

"Then why did you grab my arm and start to run like that? Why are you shaking? People don't act like that if there's nothing the matter!"

"I don't know. I swear it—I don't know!"

He *was* shaking, and his heart was pounding against

his chest. Before him, the girl's face was a dark blur, raised to his own. Impulsively, he bent his head and brought his mouth down hard upon hers. It was not a gentle kiss; it was desperate and frightened, a crying out through the darkness for something, someone.

When he raised his head, there was a sob in his throat.

"Joan," he said chokingly, "I don't know what to do! I don't know who to turn to! Joan, I'm scared! I'm starting to remember things, but they're the *wrong* things! They don't fit! Nothing fits!"

The girl in his arms was silent a moment.

Then she said, "There's one thing you're certainly not remembering. I'm Peggy. Peggy Richards. Not *Joan*."

Fourteen

The apartment was dark when Dave entered.

He stood for a moment in the doorway, listening to the steady breathing of the other occupant. He had known Lance was home, for he had seen the Volkswagen parked by the curb outside the building, but he had not been prepared to find him sleeping.

Now, suddenly, he was aware of how very late it was, of the miles he had walked along the waterfront after seeing Peggy home. She had been so hurt. That had been the terrible part, seeing the pain in her face, hearing the flat note in her voice when she said, "Well, if you won't tell me, Dave, you won't. I certainly can't make you. Certainly you don't *owe* me any explanations."

"It's not that I don't want to tell you, Peg," he had answered miserably. "It's that I can't. I don't understand myself. I have to be alone—to think."

"All right, *be* alone if that's what you want. I don't have to sit around waiting for you. Like you've told me yourself, there are plenty of fun things happening at the university—dances, parties, all sorts of things."

She had thrown the words out at him in an angry rush, and then seemed more upset when he nodded in agreement.

"Sure there are, Peg. That's what I've been telling you. You *ought* to be going to those things."

She had stood glaring at him for a long moment out of tear-filled eyes. Then she had whirled and walked into the house and shut the door in his face.

Now, standing in the doorway of his own apartment, Dave felt tired with a heavy weariness that was more than physical. His head ached with the strain of the effort he had been making to think, to remember. But he knew now what it was he had to do.

Determinedly he closed the door behind him and switched on the overhead light.

"Lance," he said. "Wake up."

The boy in the far bed twisted, mumbled, turned to bury his face in his pillow to escape the flood of brightness.

Dave crossed to him and put a hand on the shoulder beneath the sheet.

"Lance, wake up. I want to talk to you."

"Oh, for Pete's sake, are you nuts or something? It's the middle of the night!" The boy rolled over, squinting up against the light, his face smooth and brown against the white of the pillow. "What's the matter?"

"That's what I want to ask you. What *is* the matter?" Dave seated himself on the foot of the bed. "Lance, who is Joan?"

"Joan? How should I know who Joan is. Joan who?"

"There was a girl named Joan, back before we came out here. What I want to know is, who was she?"

Lance lay very quiet, gazing up at him. His green eyes were impenetrable.

"What makes you ask something like that? You can't remember anything. At least, you said you couldn't."

"Tonight I did. For an instant. There was this girl

Peggy, the one I've been dating. I kissed her. Then, suddenly, it was like I wasn't kissing Peggy at all. She was somebody else. She was Joan! I *called* her Joan, and I felt—all of a sudden—a lot of things! Things I'd never felt with Peggy!"

Lance seemed to be thinking hard.

Finally he said, "You did date a girl in New York. Her name might have been Joan for all I know. I didn't keep track of who you went out with. You dated a lot of different people. You had your friends and I had mine, just like we do here."

"This wasn't just a casual girl. This was somebody special. This girl meant something." Dave's voice was tight and controlled. "What's the name, Lance?"

"David. David Carter." The younger boy pulled himself to a sitting position. "I've told you that."

"Tonight, when I stopped to pick Peggy up at the place where she works, there was a girl there. A pretty girl, kind of small. She called me Dan. She couldn't have known me, of course. My back was to her. She had me mixed up with somebody. But, she called me Dan, and I turned around! *I knew the name!*" He leaned forward, his hands gripping into fists. "My name isn't David. You lied to me about that. My name is Daniel, isn't it? *Isn't it?*"

Lance was watching him carefully.

"Your name's David Carter," he said evenly. "Why should I lie about it? Dan's a nickname. Our mother used to call you that when you were real little. It was from a song, 'Danny Boy.' She used to sing it all the time. It was a favorite of hers."

Dave sat back, his fists clenched in his lap.

He said, "Prove it."

"Prove what? What do you mean?"

"Prove that my name's David Carter. I want to see some identification. I don't have anything, not a darned thing. No driver's license, no Social Security card, nothing. Where are they, Lance? They exist, they must, because I know how to drive. I must have a New York license."

When Lance did not answer, he continued.

"I've been thinking tonight about a lot of things, things I've been too befuddled to really wonder about before. The license on that Volkswagen of yours, it's not New York, it's New Mexico. How come?"

"I—I bought it there." Lance's eyes shifted from his face. "We left New York by bus. In New Mexico I picked up the car."

"What about luggage? You have clothes with you. Why don't I? I had to buy shirts and pants and stuff after we got out here, but you were all fixed up— sweaters, sports jackets, everything. Where's my stuff?"

"It was lost. Your suitcase—on the bus—"

"I don't believe you. I don't believe anything, not a darned think you've been saying." Dave's voice was controlled, but he knew that his rising rage must show on his face, for the other boy was watching him nervously, his own face drained of color. "I think you're a smooth, practiced, angel-faced liar! I want to see some identification! I want to know who I am! I want the truth! I'm bigger than you are, Lance, a whole lot bigger, and so help me, I'm going to get the truth if it means knocking you all the way across the room! What kind of game are you playing? I want to know, and I want to know *now!*"

For a moment Lance was silent. Then, slowly, he nodded.

"Okay. Okay, you asked for it. I've been trying to

look out for you. You've been sick, and I thought it would be better to play it cool for a while. You're right about your name—it's not David Carter. I made that up. Your name's Dan, just as you've guessed it is. Dan Cotwell."

"Dan Cotwell." He spoke it softly. "Yes, I'll buy that. The girl at the restaurant called me that. My gosh, she must *really* have known me before!" He paused. "Okay, I'm Dan Cotwell. Why did you give me this story about my being somebody else?"

"Don't push it, Dan, will you?" There was a note of pleading in the younger boy's voice. "Why don't you let well enough alone? Out here you're Dave Carter. Why don't you relax and *be* Dave Carter? That's what I'd hoped. It's a whole new start, a new life. Can't you just accept it?"

"No," Dan said quietly, "I can't. Whatever the story is, I want to know it, all of it. So start talking, little brother. You *are* my little brother, aren't you? Or is that a lie too? Are you Lance Carter or Lance Cotwell or what?"

The boy drew a long breath.

"Neither one." He shoved back the sheet and swung his legs over the side of the bed. "You want to see some identification. Okay, I'll get it for you. I've got it, the drivers' licenses and Social Security, for both of us."

He got up and crossed the room to the bureau, pulled open the top drawer, and rummaged for a moment among the shirts and underwear. When he turned back, he had the cards in his hands. He handed them to Dan. On the top of them was a clipping from a newspaper.

Dan studied them in silence.

Then he said, "This clipping about the two missing boys, Daniel Cotwell and Lawrence Drayfus, Jr. Those boys are us?"

"Right."

"They have us listed as dead!"

"Yes."

"Maybe," Dan said carefully, "you'd better tell me how it happened."

"You read the article," Larry said. "It's correct up to a point. We are from Las Cruces, New Mexico, we're close friends, we went on a weekend camping trip together. We never came back from it as far as the rest of the world is concerned. What actually happened is that while we were hiking you slipped and fell, hitting your head. It was a long time before you regained consciousness. In fact, you were only conscious at intervals all the way out here. Even when you were awake, you couldn't remember anything."

"But why are we here? What are we doing in California when our families think we're dead?" Dan asked in puzzlement.

"You had it planned that way," Larry told him, "before we ever went on that camping trip. You were never going home. You were coming out here to start a new life for yourself. You told me about it that weekend after we left the house and begged me to help you. I was to go back on Monday and tell them there had been a terrible accident, that you were swept into the river. You and I aren't really brothers, it's true, but we're as good as, as far as friendship goes. We've been buddies for years, Dan. You knew I'd do anything in the world for you. That's why I was so sick about . . ."

He hesitated.

157

"About what?" Dan asked grimly.

"About the trouble you were in. You started out with it, I guess, just as a way to earn some extra cash. By the time you told me about it, you were in too deep to get out again. I couldn't believe it at first, but then I saw how scared and desperate you were, and I knew it was true. You were beginning to realize that it would be just a matter of time before you got caught, and when you did it would mean jail—years and years of it. You were over eighteen. You're not a juvenile. You'd be right in there with the rest of the bunch."

"What the devil are you talking about?" Dan asked. His head was pounding. Great waves of pain swirled beneath his forehead. The room seemed blurred and out of focus as the light-haired boy continued saying the unbelievable things, the incredible things that somehow were not completely incredible at all. The ground had been wet and slippery and he had slipped—no, he hadn't actually slipped, somehow he had the feeling there had been hands on his back, a hard shove.

"You had your plan all made," Larry was continuing. "I agreed to help you as far as I could. Then when you fell, you were hurt, Dan, you were out of your head. You could no more have driven out here by yourself than you could have flown! I knew I'd have to bring you myself.

"Actually, it wasn't the sacrifice it sounds, for me, I mean. I come from a lousy home. I've never been happy there. My folks never gave a darn about me one way or the other. They were counting the days until I came of age and they could pitch me out. So I stopped by my house and picked up some clothes while my folks were out somewhere. Then we took off west."

He paused.

"I didn't want to tell you all this until you were completely well. You've had a rough time. I thought you'd be better not knowing. That way you could start all over, no strings, no regrets."

"But, why?" Dan asked the question dazedly. "Why would I plan something like this? Why would I need to get away so completely? My gosh, Larry, what did I *do?*"

"You were part of a dope ring," Larry told him solemnly. "You were helping to smuggle marijuana across the border from Mexico and were distributing it to the high school kids in Las Cruces."

"Smuggling marijuana!" Dan repeated in horror. "I couldn't have been! I'd never do a thing like that!"

"You needed cash, Dan. There's a lot of money in that sort of thing. More—a heck of a lot more—than for doing something like delivering newspapers! And you don't have to kill yourself getting up at the crack of dawn either!"

"I don't believe it!" Dan said. He pressed his hand hard against his throbbing forehead. "If only I could remember! But, I will soon—I'm bound to. Now that things have started coming back to me, they're sure to keep coming. They'll get sharper and sharper."

"Sure, they will." Larry reached over and patted his shoulder. "Say," he added in a brighter voice, "you know what our landlord did today? He had some repairmen come and fix our balcony."

"The balcony?" Dan stared at him. He did not believe he could have heard him correctly. "The landlord fixed the balcony! What's that got to do with anything?"

"Nothing, really," Larry said quietly. "I just thought you'd want to know. I mean, we can use it now. You might want to sit out there when you do your remembering."

Fifteen

Frank pulled the car into the parking lot and turned off the ignition. It was a beautiful night, some odd, disconnected corner of his mind observed ironically. The air that flowed in through the open window was fresh and cool and smelled like autumn. Over the flat, adobe-style roof of the motel, the round circle of moon stood out in the dark sky, surrounded by pinpricks of stars.

How could I not have known? Frank asked himself. It was so clear. There was so much to point to it. How could I have helped but know?

Everybody in school had heard about the marijuana party at the Brownings'. The papers had not mentioned names because the participants were juveniles, but they had published anonymous quotes from youngsters involved.

"I don't know who brought the stuff," one boy was quoted as saying. "It just sort of turned up. None of us knew it was going to be there. We just thought it was going to be another Saturday night party with Cokes and popcorn and dancing to records."

"We didn't smoke it," another student told reporters. "Would we have tried it if the cops hadn't come when they did? Gee, I don't know. I guess we might have,

161

just for a fling. There's no harm in trying anything once is there?"

The papers had made a great deal of that answer.

The question that no one seemed able to resolve was, "Where did the dope come from in the first place?" There were no adults at the party; Mr. and Mrs. Browning were out for the evening and there was no chaperon. The kilo blocks of marijuana weed must have been brought in by one of the guests. But, by whom?

No wonder he had so much money in his possession, Frank thought now. There wasn't anything small-time about what Larry was doing. He wasn't duped into this the way Joan and I were; he was right in there on the ground floor, part of it all. He wasn't just hauling the stuff across the border, he was actually distributing it!

Maybe the kids at the party had truly believed that smoking marijuana "just once" would be a harmless fling. Frank had heard enough and read enough to know better. There was never anything "one time" about dope, no matter what its form. At the next party it would have been there again, except then there would have been a charge for it. Then, before long, it would not be confined to parties. Kids would be buying it privately, smoking it at home in their bedrooms, in school rest rooms, on dates in parked cars. It would become "old stuff," no longer thrilling or different. And then there would be a *new* party, at which stronger drugs would be introduced.

It would not seem like such a big step then to try these new drugs, "just for a fling." As the student at the Brownings' party had commented, "There's no harm in trying anything once, is there?" Once—and once—again, once, until there was no going back.

That first party was like bringing germs into a new

land, Frank thought. It was like planting the beginning of a disease so you could sit back and watch it grow into an epidemic. And Larry knew exactly what he was doing!

The night was sweet and still. Out on the highway beyond the motel, headlights of cars moved past in ribbons of white. Overhead, bright dots of red and green streaked across the sky and had almost disappeared from sight before the sound of a jet broke the stillness. That faded too, and there was silence again.

Well, Frank told himself, I can't put it off any longer. I have to go in.

He opened the car door, his hand lingering on the handle. Then, resolutely, he climbed out and shut the door firmly behind him. Carrying the brown paper parcel that contained the jewelry samples, he crossed the parking lot and rapped firmly at the door to number eighteen.

The door opened immediately, as though the man behind it had been standing at the open window, watching him as he sat in the parked automobile.

Mr. Brown said, "It's about time you showed up. I was beginning to get worried."

"We had some car trouble," Frank told him. "It delayed us."

"Car trouble?" The man regarded him sharply.

"Nothing serious. I was able to fix it."

Clutching the parcel tightly in his hand, Frank stepped forward into the room.

Mr. Brown cast a quick glance out into the night. "Where's Joan Drayfus?"

"I dropped her off at her house," Frank said as casually as he could. "She'd promised her dad she'd be home early."

"That's the trouble with hiring women for any kind of responsible job," Mr. Brown said with a snort of disgust. "Everybody and everything comes before the job they're being paid to do." He held out his hand for the package. "No trouble at customs, was there?"

"Not really." Frank paused. "I think they're beginning to wonder about us a little though. We've been through so often lately, they recognize our names. It must seem funny for kids our age to keep going down and coming back all the time."

"They didn't ask you questions?" Mr. Brown asked.

"No."

"Well, that's good. Not that there was anything you couldn't have answered. Still, you're probably right about their beginning to notice you. Maybe it's time to switch to somebody else for this delivery work."

As he talked he was unknotting the string around the package. He opened the paper and took out the three silver pins.

"Did you have a chance to get a real look at these?"

"No," Frank said. "Not really."

"Well, come over here and take a gander. Then sit down. I have something to discuss with you. Another kind of business proposition, since your value in this one seems to be about over."

He spread the pins out on the bed, and Frank slowly crossed the room and stood gazing down at them. They were shiny and decorative, but ordinary in design and clumsy in construction. It seemed absurd to him now that he had ever allowed himself to conceive of anyone's taking the pain to import and copy them.

He raised his eyes to find Mr. Brown watching him closely.

"Well, Frank, what do you think of them?"

"They're—pretty," Frank said awkwardly.

"Sure they are. Anything made out of silver is 'pretty.' The Indian stuff is pretty too, don't you think? Is this any prettier? Come on, be honest!"

"No, I guess it isn't." Frank shifted nervously from one foot to the other. What was the man trying to say to him, or to get *him* to say? "I don't know much about jewelry. I'll take your word for it that this is designed better. I guess New York shops would pay more for this."

"That's ridiculous," Mr. Brown said firmly. "They'll take this and pay the same thing for it. You're not a dumb kid, Frank, or at least you don't seem to be. Do you mean to tell me you've never had the slightest doubts about the value of this junk jewelry?"

"Well, I *have* wondered—it didn't look so special— but then, like I said, I don't know enough about jewelry to be a judge of it." He braced himself and met Mr. Brown's eyes squarely. "What are you trying to tell me? There must be a point to this, but I don't seem to be getting it."

"You will, Frank. You will." Mr. Brown gestured toward a chair. "Sit down. I think it's time that you and I had a little talk."

Frank moved to the indicated armchair and lowered himself into it. He felt suddenly grateful for the support beneath him, as his knees were unaccountably weak. What was this all about?

"I'm glad the Drayfus girl isn't with you tonight," Mr. Brown began. "Girls are fine in their place, but, as I mentioned before, their place isn't in the world of business. It takes a man, with a man's logic, to understand what a real business opportunity is. Larry Drayfus was that kind of young man. He had a sharp business sense, a lot of ambition." He paused. "How about you, Frank? Are you ambitious?"

"I don't know," Frank said. "I guess I might be."

"That's what I thought," Mr. Brown said approvingly. "I had you pegged as a bright kid who'd like to get ahead in the world. Larry Drayfus, as you know, worked for me for some months. He had a lot on the ball, Larry did. He realized immediately that our 'import' business was a—screen, shall we say?—for other activities. It is this—other field—that brings in the real income to support our varied enterprises."

He waited expectantly. Frank asked the obvious question.

"What are these other activities?"

"We import grass," Mr. Brown said matter-of-factly. "Happy grass. What it is, actually, is the top of the female hemp plant. People roll it into cigarettes, smoke it, and they're happy. Problems—cares—they disappear. Worried about grades? Girl friends? Family problems? A couple of puffs of happy grass and the worries go up in smoke. It's wonderful stuff, Frank. Ever tried it?"

"No," Frank said slowly, "and I don't think I ever want to. If I have problems, I'd rather work them out, not just smoke a cigarette of some kind and pretend they don't exist any longer."

"You don't have to smoke it if you don't want to," Mr. Brown said agreeably. "Larry didn't. That didn't stop him from making a good bundle of money helping us sell it. That's the difficult part, the distribution. Anybody can bring the stuff across the border, but once it gets here it has to be disposed of. People have to be introduced to it before they're willing to buy it. Kids, we've found, are more receptive to trying something new if somebody their own age is the one to give it to them."

"Then, what you're suggesting," Frank said, "is that I work as a kind of go-between. You want me to go to parties and things and take the marijuana and start kids smoking it."

"That's about the sum of it," Mr. Brown said quietly. He leaned back in his chair, regarding Frank calmly through the thick lenses of his glasses. "With Larry gone, we need a replacement. We'll be willing to pay you the same kind of money we did Larry. The one difference will be, you're not going to handle any large hunks of 'company cash.' That's where we made our mistake with the Drayfus boy."

"How do you mean?" Frank asked blankly.

"Larry Drayfus was too smart. He learned too much too fast. He wasn't satisfied with being a small frog, he wanted the whole pond to himself. He may have looked like an innocent baby, but that kid was sharp as a nail. He learned the business from one end to the other the first couple of months he was with us, and then, the first chance he got, he pocketed a couple of thousand from the till and took off. That business of letting everybody think he fell in a river up in the Mogollons was engineered like a professional." There was a hint of reluctant admiration in his voice.

"You mean, you don't think he was really lost on that camping trip? You think he's alive somewhere?" Frank exclaimed.

"Darned right, I think he's alive somewhere. Not that any of us are likely to see him again. And wherever he is, that kid is using everything he learned from me to make himself a small fortune before he's twenty-one. But that's beside the point. The question now is, who do we get to fill Larry's spot with us? And the answer now is, Frank Cotwell."

"That's not the answer I get," Frank said shortly. "I don't want to get involved in this sort of thing."

"It's not a question of getting involved," Mr. Brown informed him easily. "Son, you *are* involved. You're in far too deep right now to be able to pull out without getting yourself thrown into a juvenile detention home."

"You're nuts," Frank said.

"I'm afraid not. Frank, you've been importing marijuana for us for months now. Every trip you've made across the border has been with a load of happy grass stuffed into the hubcaps of your car. Every time you've parked outside and come in here with that jewelry package, a business associate of mine has been parked alongside you. He's gotten out and removed the grass and replaced the hubcaps. He has also taken pictures of your car showing how the stuff was carried."

"You can't make me work for you if I don't want to," Frank said angrily. "I can report the whole operation to the police!"

"The only person you can report to the police," Mr Brown told him, "is yourself. You're the one who is on record as having made the trips across the border. You're the one whose car has been photographed. There are also several young people here in Las Cruces who would be willing to swear in court if necessary that you tried to get them to purchase this marijuana. You, on the other hand, have no proof of anything—where you got the hemp, or to whom you delivered it. Any investigation in Juarez will bring forth only a little novelty store, run by a poor but honest little man, struggling to support his family. Here in Las Cruces, you don't even know my real name, much less where to locate me. You aren't in a position to do very much bargaining, Frank."

"The police will believe me!" Frank said. He got to his feet, feeling the heat of his fury coursing through his body. Everything within him was urging him to reach out for this little man and smash his face halfway through his head. "They'll believe me! I'll *make* them!"

"Without proof, you won't have a leg to stand on," Mr. Brown said calmly. "By this time, the packages have been removed from the wheels of your car, so you won't have those to support your story. Face it, son, whether you think you want to be or not—you're now firmly instated in the import business!"

Frank was halfway to the door when the man spoke again. He had not moved from where he sat; his voice was gentle, as though soothing a startled child.

"You think this over, Frank. I'm sure you don't want to get yourself into trouble with the authorities. Your family has surely suffered enough this year without more problems. I'll be in touch with you soon, to get your decision."

Frank snatched at the door and wrenched it open.

My gosh, Joan, he thought wildly, what have you done to me! You were supposed to have got hold of the police by this time! They should have been here half an hour ago! Now it's too late—the stuff is out of the car—Mr. Brown will be gone! Like he says, I can quote this whole conversation till I'm blue in the face, but there won't be any proof to back it up!

He thought, Dan—oh, Dan! If it's true, what Mr. Brown says, what happened to Dan? Larry couldn't have taken him along. Nobody ever took Dan anywhere he didn't want to go! If something happened to Dan up there in the mountains, Larry *made* it happen!

Blindly, miserably, he started across the parking lot toward his car. He had almost reached it when a voice spoke softly from the shadows.

"Hi, kid. Looking for someone?"

"Who? What?" Frank stopped short.

The man moved out in front of him, and he saw the uniform.

"The window to that motel room is half open," the policeman said in a low voice. "There's a man up there with a recording device, taking down everything from inside. There are two men up there by the door ready to take your friend, Mr. Brown, when he walks out. The other one we picked up nice and easy, when he was taking the hubcaps off your car."

"Oh, gosh—oh, thank God." Frank reached out for support and found the fender of his car. "Joan did tell you!"

"In detail. It wasn't really a surprise to us. We've known something of this sort was going on. It was just a matter of pinpointing who was involved and how it was arranged."

"Will people . . ." Frank struggled for words, "will they have to know? I mean, everything? Joan's mother —she's been sick—it might be awful—"

"Don't worry, Frank. We're not going to see innocent people hurt if we can help it. Joan told us about her mother."

The policeman had his arm now and was opening the car door.

"Get in and sit down. You've had quite an evening. Just sit there and get hold of yourself for a few minutes. We can see the action from here."

"Great," Frank said grimly. "I'll enjoy every minute of it."

He sank into the car seat and directed his eyes toward the door of number eighteen.

Sixteen

As she left the plane and moved with the crowd through the covered tunnel into the Los Angeles Airport, Joan found that her legs felt weak beneath her and the hand that clutched her brown leather traveling purse was trembling.

The tension had been building inside her ever since she had left New Mexico. For hours she had sat quiet and alone in the seat of the plane, staring out at the heavy mattress of clouds, reliving the telephone conversation over and over again.

"I can't be sure, Joan," Anne had said, her voice shrill with excitement. "It's so incredible that I haven't known whether or not to call you. The thing is—I think I've seen Dan."

"Seen *Dan!*" Joan's own voice had been a gasp. "What do you mean, Anne? How could you?"

"Well, last Saturday I had a dinner date, and this fellow and I and another couple went to a little seafood restaurant called the Green Cove. We were late and the place was getting ready to close, with waitresses running around, wiping off tables and things, when this boy came in. I didn't see him at first—I was busy talking to my date—but then I saw this waitress smile across the room, like she knew somebody, and I glanced over

172

and he was sitting at a little table by the door. He looked so familiar, but then the place was kind of dark, with colored lights and things, and I was sure I was mistaken.

"It wasn't until we got up to leave that it really hit me. I was standing at the door, waiting for my date to pay the bill, and the boy came over to pay *his* bill, and—Joan, I could swear he was Dan!"

"But how could that be?" Joan exclaimed.

"I don't know. I can't explain it. I *know* Dan, Joan. I dated him before he started going with you! It's not like he was just a casual acquaintance. This boy had the same walk, the same way of holding his head, the same smile! It was like seeing a ghost!"

"But did you just let him go by?" Joan asked incredulously. "Didn't you speak to him?"

"Of course! I called out his name, and he turned around! That's the part that kept me from thinking I was really crazy! When I said, 'Dan' he froze and turned his head. Then—well, he acted as though he didn't know me at all. He said I had him confused with somebody else. He had a girl with him, one of the waitresses, and he grabbed her arm and took off out the door, almost running."

"But, if it were really Dan, he wouldn't have done that," Joan said, perplexed. "He would have recognized you too."

"I don't know, Joan. Think about it a minute. If it was Dan, if he left New Mexico and came out to California and let us all think he was dead, it sounds impossible, doesn't it, but if he *did* do those things, he must have had a reason. And whatever that reason was, he wouldn't want to be found. It would be perfectly logical that he would react to his name, and then, when he saw me, pretend he hadn't."

"I . . . suppose so." Joan's heart was pounding. "I can't believe it. I mean, I believe *you*—I know you wouldn't call me with something like this unless you really thought it was true—but, oh, Anne, how could it be?"

"I can't figure it out any better than you can," Anne said, "and as I say, I'm not sure. I can't be. But you would be! If you saw him, you'd *know!*"

"Yes!" Joan's hand tightened on the receiver.

"Come on out here, Joan! I'll meet you at the airport. We talked about your coming before I ever left Las Cruces. Your dad won't think it's strange. Just tell him I called and renewed the invitation."

"Yes. Yes, I will," Joan said. "I'll call and make reservations right away. I'll telegraph you when to expect me."

It was crazy, of course—absolutely crazy. It couldn't be Dan. And yet, if it were! She replaced the receiver on the hook, knowing that she could no more stay at home now than she could have taken the photograph by her bed and dropped it into the wastebasket. In her heart, Dan was alive, as alive as he had ever been. Steady and strong, he had stayed with her no matter how firmly she had told herself that he was gone forever. It was not a refusal to accept reality, as it had been with her mother. She had accepted with her mind the fact of the boys' deaths, but deep below consciousness, somewhere in the heart of her, a spark of hope had flickered still. She knew that now—she could admit it! It had taken something as positive as Anne's phone call to set the spark into a blaze of flame!

She did not tell Frank. It would have been too cruel

to have built up hopes, which would, in all probability, be shattered. Besides, his mind was completely occupied with the excitement of being asked to give testimony against John Brown, whose name, it turned out, was Thomas Lupino. The hearing was to take place in closed court with the names of all minors involved kept out of the papers.

To her father she said only that Anne had invited her to come spend a week in California.

"It sounds like a good plan," Mr. Drayfus said immediately. "I couldn't be more in favor. Visit with Anne, see the campus, go to some football games and dances and things. You need the break, Joan. With your mother coming home in a couple of weeks, you're going to be tied down here for a while."

There had been no problem about reservations—no problem about anything. She had withdrawn money from her savings account to purchase a ticket, put a few clothes in a suitcase, and the next moment, it seemed, she was at the airport.

"Have fun, honey!"

"I will, Daddy!"

For a moment she had clung to him hard, wishing she could tell him, but knowing that she must not. All the common sense she had told her that this was impossible, a wild-goose chase leading nowhere.

Anne is bound to be wrong, she told herself over and over. She admits she wasn't close and the place wasn't well lighted. Many people resemble each other. Mother took Frank for Dan right in the broad light of day. There are lots of tall, freckled, cinnamon-haired young men in the world.

How could it be Dan? Why should he be in California? How could he do a thing like this to his family—to me—to himself? And if Dan is there, what about Larry—might he be there also? Could they both be safe, both here in Los Angeles, somehow, through some miracle?

Now, standing at the end of the tunnel, she glanced about her, lost in the crowd that seethed in all directions. How could anyone locate a single face among so many? If one of those faces should be Dan's, would she even know it?

A sense of panic filled her, and she clutched her purse more tightly against her side.

A light, clear voice called her name, and a moment later Anne was there beside her, her arms around her in a tight hug.

"Oh, Joanie, I'm so glad you came!"

"Oh, Anne!" Joan clung tightly to her friend. Now, suddenly, seeing the familiar face, the immense reality of the situation swept over her. Anne was not a dreamer, a clinger to wishes! Anne was sensible and down to earth and always had been. If Anne was sure enough to telephone and ask her to come here, her reasons must be good ones.

"Have you found out any more?" Joan asked breathlessly. "Have you seen him again?"

"No, not the boy himself, but I have a lead to him. I went by the Green Cove last night and described the girl, the one he was with, to the manager. Her name is Peggy Richards. She wasn't there when I went by, she goes to college in the daytime and works just weekends, but she should come on duty today at four. We can catch a cab and go over there right now!"

There was not going to be any more time.

The realization was heavy and complete. It came

with the same certainty and sense of finality that the other realization had, back in Las Cruces, that spring day when he had known beyond a doubt that he would have to go, that the time was right, the situation perfect.

That's the thing that so many people can't seem to understand, Larry Drayfus thought. There has to be a sense of timing. You have to have a feel for the time when things are right and act then, not later. Later is too late.

Like Dan's mind, for instance. It was clearing. It was coming back quickly, much more quickly than he had ever imagined it would. Since that night less than a week ago when he had remembered Joan's name, the light within him had been growing brighter. He had seemed to accept, at first, the things that Larry had told him:

"How could I?" he had asked in agonized confusion. "How could I have gotten involved in anything like that!"

"It wasn't that bad," Larry had told him. "My gosh, it wasn't as though you murdered somebody. Somebody was going to cart the stuff across the border. Somebody was going to distribute it. If it hadn't been you, it would have been any of a dozen other guys."

"Am I really the kind of person who could think that way!" Dan had exclaimed. "Could I start kids out on a life of mind-wrecking drugs without even a qualm of guilt! What kind of creature am I?" His voice had been grim. "And if I am that sort of guy, why did I want to run away? Why didn't I just sit there smugly raking in the cash?"

"Things closed down on you," Larry said. "You were at a party that got raided. You had brought the stuff over and were just getting ready to leave. Nobody had even started on it yet, when suddenly the police walked in. The whole gang was hauled down to the police station, you among them. Nobody realized you were the source of the stuff, you were just another unsuspecting guest. You would have got off free and clear just like the others if it hadn't been for your dad."

"My dad?" Dan asked. "What did he do? Did he know I was responsible for the drugs being there?"

"No, but that didn't make any difference, not to him. He decided you had to be sent away to keep you from associating with evil elements! To military school, yet! Can you imagine marching around a drill field in a cute little uniform, having to be in bed at ten o'clock every night, doing KP duty—good grief, it would have been just like the Army! A whole year of that! A whole year, gone out of your life!"

His voice shook with bitterness.

Dan was staring at him.

"He must have loved me, to care that much about what became of me."

"Love you!" Larry said coldly. "Don't fool yourself. Your dad took pleasure out of making your life miserable. He never let you do anything. Your mom was just as bad in another way. She was a fool, always hanging onto you, treating you like you were a baby. And you had a sister too, a Goody-goody Two-shoes, big as a horse—the efficient kind who always wanted to run everything. You were right in taking off when you did. You were well out of that dumb family."

Dan had seemed to accept it then. Now, however, most of a week had passed. Each new day seemed to be drawing his mind upward.

There were times when Larry found the other boy watching him, a strange look in his eyes.

There were questions:

"You're sure I didn't have a brother? Or, maybe, two brothers? It seems to me there was somebody I used to talk to—to kid around with."

"My mother—what did she look like? Where did my dad work?"

"That camping trip—I remember, it was raining. The rocks were slippery, but somehow I don't think that was the reason I fell. There was something that *made* me fall—something that fell against me or bumped me or something."

Time was growing short. It was coming back too quickly now, gathering momentum like a stream, starting slowly and then moving from its original trickle into a rushing downhill current. It would not take much now to cause the gates to break wide and memory to come flooding back in its entirety.

Would he remember the hands upon his back, shoving him forward? It had seemed so simple there on the cliff above the river. One boy's body would be found and the other not; the natural assumption would be that both had fallen into the swollen river.

Except, it had not worked that way. Dan had fallen, yes, but he had rolled against a boulder, not over the edge of the bank. When Larry reached him he had been sitting up, gazing dazedly about him.

"What happened?" he had asked dumbly. "Who are you?"

Larry had dropped to his knees beside him.

"Dan," he had begun—but the other boy's eyes had been blank.

"Don't you know who I am?" Larry had asked softly.

"No," Dan had said, and pain had swept across his face like a screen, masking off everything else.

There had been nothing to do, then, but take him along. He could not leave him, for he would not have died there, not a hulk like Dan Cotwell. There was something in Dan that carried him through everything that ever happened to him. A fall that bad would have finished anyone else, but there was Dan, sitting on the ground, wiping the mud from his face, struggling through the pain to ask, "What happened?" He could not be left there to be found alive to tell his stumbling story of "a fellow who pushed me and went off and left me." There was no choice but to take him along.

They had climbed slowly and painfully back up the bluff to the road, where a little gray Volkswagen was parked in just the place that Larry had seen it the day before, with the keys left conveniently above the windshield. Once inside, Dan had passed out on the back seat. It had been a simple thing to stop at the Drayfus house and collect some clothing and the money, which had been stored in a wallet under the mattress, to stop on the far side of town to exchange license plates with a rundown car parked on a side road, to tell Dan when he sat up, groaning softly, "Lie down. Lie back. You've been sick. You need to rest."

"Who? Where?"

"You're David Carter," Larry had told him, drawing the name at random because of the initials. "I'm your brother, Lance. We're from New York. You've been sick. Now lie back and get some sleep."

How simple it had been! How gloriously simple! And it had worked out better than he had ever dared hope. Once here in California, it was Dan who had found a job with which to support them both. For Larry it had been like one long vacation, with no school, no pressures, no one telling him what to do and how to do it. Then, recently, he had met those fellows at one of the surfing parties. He had let them know in a subtle way that, regardless of his appearance, he wasn't an innocent baby. He had been involved in some big business back where he came from, and out here on the Coast it was even bigger. A guy could make as much money as he wanted, depending upon the risks he was willing to take, particularly a guy who looked like Larry, with an innocent, childlike face, big eyes, a heart-wrenching smile.

And beyond that—who knew what life might hold! This was just the beginning! There would be bigger, more exciting games always to come!

The thing was that Dan could not be a part of them. Dan must not be allowed to remember more than he already did. He had almost laughed aloud when Dan had asked him about his own family. They were nothing to him; they never had been. What did he have in common with people like that? In some freak way he had found himself among them, like an eagle being born into a cuckoo's nest.

There was only one person in the world that Larry Drayfus was concerned about, and that was Larry Drayfus. Or Lance Carter. Or whoever it was that it was convenient to be at the moment.

"Dan?"

Across the room from him, the older boy looked up. There was a hint of suspicion in his eyes.

"What is it?"

Larry got up slowly and walked over to the French doors, unsealed now, leading onto the balcony.

"Come over here a minute, will you?" he said. "I want to point something out to you."

"Daniel Cotwell." The girl in the white waitress uniform repeated the name carefully. She stared at Anne, recognition dawning in her eyes. "You were here the other night, weren't you? You're the girl who called out to Dave?"

"Dave?" Joan caught at the name. "Who is Dave?" Is that the name of the boy you were with?"

"David Carter. He's the boy I've been dating."

The girl transferred her attention from Anne to Joan, studying her with wide gray eyes. She had a familiarity about her, Joan thought in surprise—the shape of the face, the way the eyes were spaced, the wide mouth with even teeth.

Have I seen her some place before, she asked herself. No, I can't have, of course. Then why does she seem so familiar? Perhaps she looks like someone.

The thought was disturbing. If this strange girl, whom she knew she could not possibly have set eyes on before, could call forth such a strong feeling of recognition, might not a boy built like Dan, with features like his and his walk and smile, have drawn this same response from Anne?

"Can you tell us anything about this David?" she asked.

The girl, Peggy, said, "Why? What is it exactly that you want to know, and why? I can't just tell you things without knowing why you want to hear them."

"There was a boy," Joan said, "a friend of ours named Dan Cotwell. Four months ago he went on a camping trip in the Mogollon Mountains. He never came back. The other night, here at the Green Cove,

Anne thought she saw him. It was the boy who was with you, the one you call Dave. Of course, she could very well be wrong."

"Where are the Mogollon Mountains?" Peggy asked.

"In New Mexico, outside of Las Cruces."

"Dave is from New York. At least he said he was." She paused. "He wouldn't lie. I can't imagine his lying. Even last weekend when I got so mad at him, he didn't try to tell me things that weren't so just to smooth things over."

"You had a fight last weekend?" Anne asked. "Was this after I spoke to him?"

"Yes. It was strange—he acted so peculiar. Everything had been fine, and then, just as we were getting ready to leave, you said something to him, and he grabbed hold of me and practically yanked me out the door. He was very upset about something. I tried to ask him about it and he told me he didn't know himself what was wrong. Then he stopped walking and he . . . he . . ."

She let the sentence fall away.

"Yes?" Joan prodded eagerly.

"He—he called me by somebody else's name. Joan. He called me Joan."

They were all silent a moment. Peggy's eyes were dark with remembered pain. She raised them slowly with a look of dawning understanding.

"You're Joan," she said softly, "aren't you?"

Silently, Joan nodded.

"He lives at the Royal Palm Apartments," Peggy told her. "I—I'd go over with you, but I can't leave work right now. I'll give you the address though."

"We'll find it," Joan said. "Thank you. Thank you so very much!"

"Tell him something for me, will you?" Peggy said. "Tell him I have a date tomorrow night to the homecoming dance. I can't get off work for the game, but I'm going to the dance afterward. I'm going with a real great fellow—a living doll! Besides that, he drives a Karmann Ghia."

She turned away quickly, her head bent forward so that her face was hidden. She held her body carefully erect.

She was tall.

With a sudden flash, Joan realized where she had last seen Peggy Richards. She was gazing out at her from her own mirror.

The girl on the sidewalk below the balcony was not Peggy. He had thought she was when he first saw her, but now he realized that it was someone quite different. She was looking down, pawing through her purse for change to tip the cab driver, but then she straightened and he knew her as completely as he had ever known anyone in his life.

It was Joan Drayfus.

For a moment he stood staring. Then he turned to find Larry close behind him. Too close. When had he moved so close?

"You're a rotten little liar," Dan said softly.

Larry's face was a mask of innocent surprise.

"Why do you say that?"

"Those things you told me, they were lies, every one of them! I was never involved in narcotics smuggling! I didn't hate my parents! I didn't even have a sister! The things you were telling me about myself, they were true, all right, but not about *me!* It was you —*you!*"

"You're crazy," Larry said. "You can't remember everything just like that, when just a few minutes ago——"

"I do remember," Dan told him. He felt weak with the knowledge, the sudden surge of violent memory. The gates had opened; pictures were pouring in one great rush back into his brain.

"I do remember, because Joan is here, right here in front of this building right now! It's Joan—my girl! Your sister! I *remember!*"

To have ever forgotten, that was the incredible thing! Not the return of memory, but the fact that he had ever been without it! Joan, her head tossed back, laughing at some silly joke he had made—Joan bent over a geometry book, brow wrinkled in concentration—Joan, tall and stately, yet still with the endearing shyness of a little girl, raising a beaming face from the corsage he had given her for that Christmas formal, how long ago? Two years?

It had been their first date. He had not known then what she would become to him. He had not even guessed. She was a casual date, a third-choice invitation because Anne was already dated up and the next girl he called was also. He had waited too long, so he had better get on the ball and call someone right away. Why not Joan Drayfus? She was a nice kid, popular with everyone but not glamorous. She didn't date much; she would probably be free.

"It's beautiful," she had said.

It wasn't really. It was a little on the wilted side, that carnation corsage, thrown together at the last moment by a harried florist who had already put together a hundred Christmas corsages. Most girls would have found it disappointing, but Joan's eyes had been shining.

"It's beautiful, Dan!"

She had lifted it to her face and suddenly, startlingly, *she* had been beautiful, so aglow with life and happiness that his heart had lifted in a quick rise of wonder.

That he could have forgotten the dreams, the plans! They had both been planning on college, so there had not been anything definite. Not yet. But they had both known. Gloriously, unspokenly—there had been no doubt, ever, of what was between them and what would someday be.

How could he have forgotten, even for an instant, much less for months! What was it now, October? The college year had already started! They had been here in California since spring! He had missed it all—exams—graduation—the prom! His parents—dear God, what about his family! Were they frantically searching for him? Or did they think he was dead? That newspaper clipping—how could they think anything else!

"You—you—" He could not find a word strong enough.

"I guess you do remember at that." Larry was regarding him warily. "Well, what are you going to do about it? Are you going to tell them?"

"Tell them? How can I not? Do you really think I'm going to stay here, lolling on the beach, now that I know who I am!"

"No, of course not! You'll go on back. You'll tell them you had a crack on the head and got amnesia just like it happens in books. Everybody will cheer and throw confetti—high school football hero returns from the dead! But that doesn't mean you have to tell them about me."

Larry's voice was gentle and persuasive.

"I'm not going back to New Mexico, Dan, not now or ever. Larry Drayfus doesn't exist any longer, and I like it that way. I'm free to live my own life in my own way without having to answer to anyone. Why spoil it? Why mess it up? What is it going to gain you?"

"Your folks—they must be crazy with grief!" Dan exclaimed. "Don't you even care?"

"They'll be adjusted by now. They'll have all kinds of sticky sweet memories about me. Are you going to yank those away from them? What are you going to tell them—that little Larry-boy is a monster of some kind? They won't thank you for that, Dan, I can tell you. You won't be doing them any favor. You'll give my dad a heart attack. You might give Mother one too, who knows?"

"You don't care about them," Dan said. "Why should that matter to you?"

"It doesn't. But it matters to *you*. *You* care."

"Not enough to let you get away with this!" Dan's fury was so great that he could hardly choke out the words. "Not enough to leave you running loose in the world! My Lord, if you're like this at seventeen, what are you going to be when you're twenty-seven! Or thirty-seven! Or fifty!"

"Okay. Don't say I didn't give you a chance!"

The boy shot toward him before he even saw what was happening. The hands were outstretched, the lean, wiry body had the speed of quicksilver, the smooth childlike face was twisted with a cold hard brightness. It was so sudden that his mind could not register and react, but his body could—for his body remembered. His body had lived this before!

That shove in the mountains had carried him forward over the cliff's edge, but he had been facing away, he had not been ready. Now the strong, well-trained body, so used to instant responses to football signals, threw itself sideways out of the way of the rushing figure. The boy went past him and struck the balcony railing and continued through it, out beyond it in a clean arc through the sweet blue air, silhouetted against the white breakers with their cargo of surfers, arms stretched wide like a thin brown bird.

"Oh, no!" Dan whispered the words. He could not move, he could not think. He could only stand, staring at the shattered railing.

In the street below people were screaming. Their voices rose shrilly against the pounding of his head.

"A doctor," somebody cried, and someone else: "Too late—nothing can be done."

Joan! He saw her again in his mind as he had seen her in fact only moments before, on the sidewalk beneath the balcony. Could she still be there? No—no—that would be too ironic, too impossibly cruel. Still, where would she have gone in such a short time! Could she be standing now, gazing down at her brother, or at whatever thing her brother now was!

"Oh, please no!"

He was across the room in three swift strides, throwing open the door, tearing down the hallway. He did not stop at the elevator but ran for the stairs, his feet hitting them with a crashing violence.

She was there in the lobby. She had been looking at the names on the mailboxes. Anne was with her, and they both looked up at once and saw him, their eyes widening, their faces gone white.

"Joan!" he cried, and reached her and caught her to him with a gasp that came out like a sob.

"Dan, is it you? Is it really?"

Her voice—he remembered her voice, the feel of her in his arms, the smell of her hair. She asked no questions. She merely clung to him as though there were no questions of importance that had not already been answered.

He held her there, her face pressed against his shoulder, while a man came running in from outside to use the telephone.

"Operator, get me the closest hospital! Ambulance service! Not that it will help any." He turned to them while waiting for the connection. "It's that young kid from third floor A, Lance Curtis or something. He must have been out on the balcony leaning on the railing! Fool kid! Everybody in the building knows about those balconies! Repair work was scheduled to start on them next week."

"From the third floor!" Anne's eyes were wide with horror. "Lance Curtis? Dan, was he someone you knew?"

"No," Dan said, "not really. I don't think anybody in the world ever really knew him."

Keeping Joan held close against him, he put his arm around Anne as well, turning both girls from the lobby entranceway toward the side door.

"Let's get out of here," he said hoarsely. "Let's go home."

GREAT READING FOR YOUNG ADULTS
FROM AVON ⬡ BOOKS

NORMA KLEIN

☐	Give Me One Good Reason	51292	$2.25
☐	It's Not What You Expect	43455	$1.50
☐	Mom, the Wolfman and Me	49502	$1.75
☐	Sunshine	33936	$1.75
☐	Taking Sides	41244	$1.50

RICHARD PECK

☐	Don't Look and It Won't Hurt	45120	$1.50
☐	Dreamland Lake	30635	$1.25
☐	The Ghost Belonged to Me	42002	$1.50
☐	Representing Superdoll	47845	$1.75
☐	Through A Brief Darkness	42093	$1.50

WALTER DEAN MYERS

☐	Fast Sam, Cool Clyde and Stuff	45294	$1.50
☐	It Ain't All for Nothin'	47621	$1.75
☐	Mojo and the Russians	41814	$1.50

Where better paperbacks are sold or directly from the publisher.
Include 50¢ per copy for postage and handling: allow 4-6 weeks for
delivery.

Avon Books, Mail Order Dept.
224 West 57th Street, New York, N.Y. 10019

YA 6-80

"AN AMAZEMENT . . . ENCHANTING
. . . ELECTRIFYING."
The New York Times

"MAY BE A CLASSIC FOR READERS
NOT YET BORN."
Philadelphia Inquirer

"TO READ IT IS TO FLY"
People Magazine

THE NATIONALLY ACCLAIMED NOVEL BY
WILLIAM WHARTON

NOW AN AVON PAPERBACK 47282 $2.50

AVON BOOKS PRESENTS
THE BEST IN MYSTERY & SUSPENSE
FOR YOUNG READERS

Devil By the Sea by Nina Bawden	37671	$1.50
Dreamland Lake by Richard Peck	39635	$1.25
The Ghost Belonged To Me by Richard Peck	42002	$1.50
Johnny May by Robbie Branscum	28951	$1.25
The Killing Tree by Jay Bennett	44289	$1.50
The Mystery Book Mystery by Wylly Folk St. John	47910	$1.75
The Nightmares of Geranium Street by Susan Shreve	42887	$1.50
Some Things Dark and Dangerous Ed. by Joan Kahn	36038	$1.50
Some Things Fierce and Fatal Ed. by Joan Kahn	32771	$1.50
Some Things Strange and Sinister Ed. by Joan Kahn	36046	$1.50
Toby, Granny and George by Robbie Branscum	33571	$1.25
Two For Survival by Arthur Roth	44651	$1.50

MYS 6-80